# THE PENCIL FAMILIES

Other books by Susan Terris

WHIRLING RAINBOWS *(Doubleday)*
PLAGUE OF FROGS *(Doubleday)*
PICKLE *(Four Winds Press)*
THE DROWNING BOY *(Doubleday)*
ON FIRE *(Doubleday)*
AMANDA, THE PANDA, AND
THE REDHEAD *(Doubleday)*
THE BACKWARDS BOOTS *(Doubleday)*
THE UPSTAIRS WITCH AND
THE DOWNSTAIRS WITCH *(Doubleday)*

# The Pencil Families

SUSAN TERRIS

GREENWILLOW BOOKS

A Division of William Morrow & Company, Inc. | New York

Inquiries should be addressed to Greenwillow Books, William Morrow & Company, Inc., 105 Madison Ave., New York, N.Y. 10016
Printed in the United States of America.

1 2 3 4 5 79 78 77 76 75

**Library of Congress Cataloging in Publication Data**

Terris, Susan. The pencil families.
SUMMARY: After she discovers a dead body floating in the lagoon, ten-year-old Emily's life becomes even more exciting than the fantasies she creates for her "pencil families."
[1. Brothers and sisters—Fiction] I. Title.
PZ7.T276Pe [Fic] 75-10597
ISBN 0-688-80018-1 ISBN 0-688-84018-3 lib. bdg.

For Peggy and Henry
And for Henry's boys—
Bill, Bob, and Jimmy

# 1

"Why can't I find a pencil? Where are all the pencils? What does a person have to do around here to find something to write with? Any stubby little chewed-up pencil will do. Just something that will *write!*"

That was Lawrence yelling, Emily Mendle's brother Lawrence. Most of the time he didn't even seem to see Emily, didn't even admit that her ten-year-old self lived in his house and was related to him. Only when he couldn't find a pencil. Then he yelled a lot. Emily loved to hear him yell.

"Emily! Blast it, Emily, Ma is on the phone—long distance from Oregon—and I need a pencil to take down the number of her new motel. A pencil, you idiot! *A pencil!*"

Emily frowned because she knew she was going to have to give Lawrence a pencil, a member of one of her pencil families, and this was going to cause trouble with the families. They wouldn't like having someone missing, just when they were all getting ready for their first annual spring picnic and swim on Mount Tamalpais.

This kind of decision always bothered Emily. Which

family was going to have to make the sacrifice? The Ticonderogas? The Choices? The Eagles? The Dixons? The Eberhard-Fabers? Right now they were all lined up at the edge of the kitchen sink watching the pencil babies at their swimming lessons. Tall father pencils, medium-sized mother pencils, and shorter brother and sister pencils. As Emily was staring down at the little baby ones floating in the kitchen-sink pool, a gigantic hand reached out and snatched the Eagles' baby from the water.

"Kidnapped!" cried the Eagle-family mother. "My baby Lucinda's been kidnapped. Help! Help!"

"Don't worry," Emily assured her. "I'll get your child back." Quickly she fished the rest of the babies out of the water, threw them into a dishtowel with the other pencils, and ran down the hall to her room. "Hide here," she told the pencil families, shoving them under the mattress on her bed, "and I'll rescue Lucinda after I talk to Ma."

Then she rushed back to her parents' bedroom and grabbed the extension phone. "Ma, Ma," she cried breathlessly, "Lawrence just stole the Eagles' baby. You said he couldn't take my family members without permission, didn't you? If he'd asked nicely, I would have gone to my room and gotten him one of the pencil orphans. Come home, Ma. You've been gone a month already. I miss you. Do you *have* to study oceanography?"

Lawrence was still on the other phone and his fourteen-year-old voice was so loud and deep that he drowned her out when he spoke up again. "I can't ever find a pencil. I'm spending all my baby-sitting money on pencils that I have to hide, and she still finds them and steals them."

"Pipe down, Lawrence," his mother said amiably. "Do let Em talk for a minute."

Emily started in right away. "Ma, Lawrence doesn't *see* me. He doesn't *hear* me. I'm so lonely—especially this last week when Daddy's been in L.A. Come home. I have to keep looking in the bathroom mirror to make sure I'm still here."

Emily's mother, Joan Mendle, laughed. Then in a kind and patient mother-voice that was comfortably far-off in Oregon, she reminded Emily that she'd be home in one more week. Next she told Lawrence to be more considerate and Emily to stop taking pencils. After that she tried to change the subject. "What did you do, Em, for your first two days of spring vacation?"

"Yesterday Carla and I collected shells at the beach and today we went hiking on Mount Tam."

"Well, that was fun, wasn't it?"

Forgetting that her mother couldn't see her, Emily

nodded her head. "Yeah, but the rest of the time—dinner and at night—is so boring without you. There's nothing to do but watch TV and answer all the calls from people who want to send telegrams. Why did Western Union need a new telephone number? And why did they pick one just like ours? And listen, Ma, on the TV news they keep telling about houses here at Stinson and Bolinas that have been robbed. Doesn't that make you worry about us? Doesn't that make you think you should come home?"

"Are you practicing the piano?" her mother asked. "Is Nettie treating you all right?"

"Yes . . . fine, fine," Emily agreed. "I like Nettie. She's funny. She tells wonderful stories about things that happened to her—or almost happened. Did you know she used to live in Hollywood and had a chance to be in a movie? But her sister got sick and she had to come up here to take care of her. Isn't that too bad? But, Ma—even if I do like Nettie—I still miss *you!*"

As Emily spoke, she waved and smiled at Nettie who was sitting at the sewing machine in her parents' room. Nettie Hartman—crazy Nettie—her father's cousin's sister-in-law who had agreed to move from her apartment in San Francisco to their hillside house at Stinson Beach and look after them for five weeks while Joan Mendle was up in Oregon studying.

"Everything else is all right then?" Joan Mendle asked. "Emily?"

"Yeah, I'm here. I guess so. At least Daddy will be home from Los Angeles tomorrow night."

There was a long silence on the line from Oregon. Then Emily's mother spoke again. This time her voice sounded tired and less patient. "Well, actually, that's why I called . . ."

Emily didn't listen carefully after that. Just enough to realize that her father was not returning home from his business trip. Instead, he was flying directly to Oregon to join her mother for six days. That would leave Emily alone with Nettie and Lawrence for her whole vacation. It was going to be an awful vacation, she decided, as she hung up the phone. Awful and boring.

An hour later, still brooding, Emily sat down at the table in the big room which served the Mendles as kitchen, dining room, and living room. She stared across the table at Nettie, watching her lay out tissue-paper pattern pieces on a length of brightly colored fabric. Emily noticed that Nettie was wearing a new fuschia-and-white Hawaiian flowered muu-muu, and that her red hair was braided this evening into two long pigtails, each tied at the bottom with a paper ribbon that said See's Candy.

Emily didn't have to look at Lawrence because she knew just what he was doing. He was over by the front window, seated at the desk, peering at something on a slide under his microscope. He was working on a plankton project he was about to submit for a competition at the Academy of Sciences in San Francisco. Emily frowned in his direction. Even when he wasn't working on a special project, he spent half of his time bent over the microscope.

Looking back at Nettie, Emily stared and stared—at the arcs of wrinkles in the corners of her eyes, at the bulge of her Adam's apple, at the brown splotches on the backs of her hands. Then, at last, she asked a question. "How old are you, Nettie?"

"Young enough to have missed Halley's Comet the last time and young enough to expect to see it when it comes back again."

"When will that be?" Emily asked, noticing newly cut flowers arranged in a jar sitting at one end of the table.

"Nineteen-eighty-four," Nettie said, as she began pinning one piece of the tissue to her green and yellow cloth. "Or is it nineteen-eighty-six?"

Because Emily was bored doing nothing but watching Nettie, she tried drumming her fingernails on the table, hoping that the noise would annoy Lawrence and make him look up. It didn't.

"See how long I'm growing my fingernails, Nettie? I'm not going to cut them until Ma comes home. Hey, fingernails remind me of toenails. Do you know why elephants paint their toenails purple?"

Nettie smiled with a mouthful of color-tipped straight pins. Then she spit them out. "So they can hide in grape vines," she answered smugly.

"How did you know?" Emily asked, jumping up and knocking over the wicker chair.

"I read your joke book while you were at the beach yesterday." As Nettie spoke, she kept inserting the pins. In-out-in, Emily noticed. Every single pin was put in that exact way.

Emily bent down and picked up the chair. "Maybe Lawrence doesn't know. Lawrence, Lawrence—why do elephants paint their toenails purple?"

There was no answer so she asked again. Still no answer. Emily sighed. "I think I'll play the piano," she mused, but on her way over to it, she paused and turned back to Nettie again. "Where did the red flowers on the table come from?" she asked. "We don't have any like that in our yard. Did you steal them?"

"Me steal?" Nettie asked, pushing her pearl-studded glasses back up on the bridge of her nose. "You'd better stop ripping off all the pencils around here before you start accusing other people. I don't steal . . . oh, yes . . . except once, I *almost* did. I almost stole some big movie star's boyfriend when I was in Hollywood. She was the lead and I was the stand-in. But then I got sick —scarlet fever—and had to drop out of the cast."

Not knowing whether to believe Nettie or not, Emily smiled, shrugged, and sat down on the piano bench. Then, with a dramatic flourish, she started to play. She did hit the right notes—most of them—but she hit them very hard. She played the "Spinning Song" over and over again. "Spinning Song" and more "Spinning Song." Spin-spin-spin with her long fingernails clicking against the piano keys. As she played, she swiveled her head to see if she was disturbing Lawrence. She wasn't. He was still staring stoop-shouldered into his microscope. He didn't even hear her playing.

But Nettie did. Emily noticed that Nettie was frowning and tugging at her left earlobe. Emily had learned in the last month that ear-tugging was a signal—a signal meaning that Nettie was about to come down with one of her migraine headaches.

Emily stopped banging. "Don't you feel well, Netts?" she asked, noticing that middle C had a big black fingerprint on it. "Am I annoying you? I'm sorry. I didn't mean to."

"It's not you, hon, just my crazy old head," Nettie answered. "Maybe . . . maybe. Well, I think I might just take a pill and a glass of ice water. I'll rest a while. Maybe . . . maybe." Her voice trailed off. "You're such a good chef, Emily hon. Maybe . . . maybe you could whip up something for Lawrence and you. For dinner, huh?"

"Sure, sure," Emily said, giving the piano one last bang.

As Nettie shuffled out of the room, still pulling nervously at her left earlobe, Emily sighed. "Lawrence, why are elephants so wrinkled? Can't you listen to me? I have something important to ask. How come Ma didn't know about Nettie's migraines? Wouldn't she be worried about us if she knew? I don't think Daddy noticed anything wrong when he was here. He must have thought Nettie liked to go to bed early, didn't he, Lawrence? Do you believe all the stories she tells? Do you?"

Lawrence still didn't answer. He was unable to notice anything, Emily decided, except the microscopic, wriggling creatures in the drop of water sucked out of the lagoon. That was all he could see and he couldn't *hear* at all.

Emily picked up the binoculars which were lying on the desk. Looking past Lawrence, out the window, down the hill, and across the highway, she could see that the tide was rising in the lagoon. The mudflats were being flooded over. A few greedy birds still lingered there, gobbling up supper. For a minute or two she focused the binoculars on a large blue heron. Then, looking beyond the lagoon, she saw the sand spit of Stinson Beach, the breaker line, the Pacific Ocean, and a hazy yellow-pink sky. There would be a luscious sunset tonight, she decided, but Lawrence wouldn't see it.

"Did you know that blue herons can't even swim?" Emily asked her brother. "Carla told me that."

Lawrence didn't answer. Making a face at him, Emily put down the binoculars and lifted up the phone. Then she dialed Carla's number. It had only been two hours since they'd come down off the side of Mount Tamalpais, the coastal mountain that rose up two thousand feet directly behind the Mendles' house, but she needed to talk to her anyway.

"Hi, Car-Car," she said. "It's me. I have something to ask you. Why are elephants so wrinkled?"

"Oh, really, Emily," Carla's half-exasperated voice said through the receiver. "Are you still into that stuff?"

"Ever try to iron one?" Emily asked, laughing and waiting for Carla to laugh, too. "Ever try to iron one?"

"Yes, I got it the *first* time," Carla said. "Is that all you called about? I really can't hang on the phone now, because Mom has agreed to be referee while Jeff and I air some of our grievances."

"Air your grievances? What's that supposed to mean? And anyway, I *did* call about something important. Ma phoned to say that Daddy's going to Oregon to be with her for a week. And while I was talking, Lawrence stole Lucinda, the Eagles' baby. Now Nettie's gone to bed, popping pills for another migraine."

"That pencil family stuff is so childish," Carla said.

"I know," Emily agreed. "But I like it. It helps me with my stories and keeps me company when Lawrence is reading or looking into his microscope. Especially now while he's getting ready for that science fair. At least Jeff talks to you."

"And beats up on me, too. Remember that. Lawrence never lays a finger on you. Now listen, Em, I've absolutely got to go, but first I'll give you some advice—tell you just what my mom would say. Do something *outrageous*. Then Lawrence will have to notice you."

"Yeah, yeah," Emily said. "Maybe I will."

As soon as she hung up, the phone started to ring. When she picked it up, she heard a woman's voice asking for Western Union. "I'm sorry," Emily said. "You dialed wrong. Our number is *just* like the new Western Union number—except for the area code. To get Western Union and send a telegram, you have to dial 800 first. Dial 800 and *then* the number."

When she thought that the woman understood, she hung up, but she had no sooner done so than the phone rang again. Emily growled at it, hoping Lawrence would reach over and pick it up. He didn't. So after six or eight rings, she grabbed it. "No," she shouted into the receiver, "I told you you have to dial 800 first. This is *not* Western Union."

The woman's voice at the other end was sweet and perplexed. "But I'm not calling Western Union. This is Mrs. McHenry. Isn't this Emily? Is your brother there?"

"Oh, yeah, sure. Lawrence!" she called in a too loud voice. "It's Mrs. McHenry about baby-sitting again. I don't know why she asks you. I'd be better."

Lawrence didn't look at Emily, only at the receiver which he took and propped up against one shoulder. His straight brown hair hung over the earpiece. First he said nothing. Then he said, "Of course. Yes. Eight's fine," and he reached for a tablet. Next, as Emily watched, he pulled a long, newly sharpened pencil out of his microscope case and started to write down the time.

It was a Choice, she noticed. A long, slim Choice pencil just waiting to be joined to her Choice family. Mrs. Choice wasn't at all happy with her present husband anyway. He'd never been quite right since Lawrence stole him and did brain surgery on him in the pencil sharpener. She knew she couldn't get hold of that pencil now, but later when Lawrence went to baby-sit, she'd liberate it.

Thinking about this plan, she started on dinner. First

she got a black iron skillet. Then she began breaking open some eggs and dropping them into a mixing bowl. She was so absorbed that half a shell fell into the gooey liquid. As she was just about to fish it out, she suddenly changed her mind. "Do something outrageous," Carla had suggested. So Emily left the half shell in the bowl, and for good measure she added another one. After that she beat the whole mess together with a wire whisk, trying to crush the eggshell into invisible little pieces.

Not very many minutes later, she and Lawrence were sitting across from one another at the dining table. Though he didn't seem to hear Emily's voice most of the time, it always reached him when it was saying, "Dinner's ready."

"You know," she told her brother, "you need a haircut."

He didn't answer. He just unfolded his paper napkin, put it in his lap, and picked up his fork.

"I've been noticing, Lawrence, you're beginning to get a moustache."

Lawrence nodded. "So are you," he answered. "How come you aren't more like your friend Laura Stiefel? You could learn a few things from her."

"Her name is *Carla*—not Laura." Emily took a small bite out of her peanut butter and jelly sandwich. Munching it quietly, she stared at Lawrence, waiting for him to begin. He had brought a crossword puzzle with him to the table and that long, thin Choice pencil. Emily sat there without saying any more. She just ate her sandwich, drank her milk, and listened to her brother eat his scrambled eggs.

"Grinch-grinch" was the sound Lawrence made as he chewed patiently through the scrambled eggs-and-shells and added notations to his puzzle. If he noticed the crunchy texture of the eggs, he didn't say anything.

"The eggshells *are* outrageous," Emily complained to the about-to-be-married Mr. Choice. "But not outrageous enough, I guess. Lawrence never notices anything. As if I don't exist."

# 2

"Come on, Emily," Carla pleaded. "Wait up. I think we forgot something."

Emily stopped pedaling and put one foot down on the ground so that the other bicycle could pull up even with hers at the edge of the lagoon highway. "What?" she asked, staring out over the pockmarked tidal mudflats.

"We didn't bring any of those little pill bottles to take water samples for Lawrence's microscope."

Emily frowned down at Carla, whose bike had pulled up next to hers. "So what? Why should I do him any favors when he never notices *anything*? He used to—before he started junior high. And even now, he's a little better when Ma's here, but with her away . . ."

"My mom says your mom is just taking courses because she's trying to find herself," Carla said. "And maybe you just think Lawrence doesn't notice anything because you notice *everything*. Too much, if you ask me. Anyway, I like your brother. He's a genius—a real genius—and I like the way he looks, too."

To get a better view of some yellow flowers blooming

at the edge of the lagoon, Emily wheeled her bike across the highway. "His nose twists to the left," she called back over one shoulder. "And his left ear sticks out farther than the right. Besides, last night he told me I'm getting a moustache. Am I?"

"Everyone has facial hair," Carla said.

Emily watched her as she wheeled her blue bicycle across the road. Carla was shorter than Emily—a pale, thin blonde with eyes just a little too close together. The eyes made her look even smarter than she was, Emily thought. And she was plenty smart enough already. Emily, on the other hand, was very ordinary. Tall for ten and strong looking, she liked to think, with shiny braces on her teeth and curly dishwater-colored hair she always wore tied back in two long tails. When her father was in a teasing mood, he would look at her face and tell her that she had a bunch of freckle families living on her nose.

This particular Monday morning the two girls were riding the six miles from Stinson Beach around the edge of the lagoon to the town of Bolinas, planning to arrive in time for the 1:37 minus tide. Emily and Carla always took turns choosing what they would do. If they didn't have some kind of organized system, Carla insisted, they'd never be able to agree on *anything*, because Carla preferred the lagoon, the beach, playing Monopoly, or drawing with felt pens. But Emily preferred hiking on the mountain, making up stories, watching TV, or cooking.

"Now that we've stopped," Carla suggested, "let's sit here and rest for a while. You always exhaust me by going too fast."

Nodding and throwing down her bike, Emily seated herself at the edge of the lagoon, with the toes of her sneakers soaking in the cold water. With one quick glance she took in flocks of gulls and coots feeding, a couple of herons, an egret, and, overhead on the electric wires, a kingfisher. The birds were making an incredible racket—cawing, peeping, croaking, quacking. The Bolinas Lagoon was a bird sanctuary, Emily knew, and people came from all over the country with fancy binoculars to study them. She wasn't interested in taking notes on it, she just liked to look—to see the birds eating and flying around over the water.

At one end of the lagoon there was an island—Kent Island. At low tide it became a peninsula and people could walk right across the mudflats to reach it. Now, as Emily looked in that direction, she saw a huge flock of gulls circling above it. When she squinted, it looked as if something strange was on the shore of the island. Near a muddy boulder, she thought she could make out a pair of fisherman's wading boots, but she wasn't sure. She'd have to check it out when they got to the other side of the lagoon.

"Want to hear the new pencil-family story I wrote last night?" she asked, grabbing a few blades of salty-tasting grass to suck on.

Carla probed around with her fingers until she found a dry spot to sit on. "Sure," she said, "if you can abbreviate it a little. Short, you know, instead of a word-for-word rerun."

Emily took a deep breath. Then she began. "Well, you see, Mrs. Susannah Choice was about to divorce her husband because of that brain surgery and because they argued when he didn't laugh at her joke about the elephant's wrinkles. But before she could divorce him, he committed suicide. He jumped off the Golden Gate Bridge."

"I thought Mrs. Choice's name was Cecelia," Carla commented.

"It was, but she changed it—legally—in court because she thought Susannah would appeal more to her new husband. He's much younger than she is, you know, but he swears it will never matter."

Carla picked up a rock and tossed it into the water, scaring off a few of the closest birds. "Honestly, Emily, all your stories sound like TV soap operas—the ones I watch when I'm sick and have to stay home from school. Those kinds of things don't happen to *real* people. Why don't you ever read any books—books other than elephant-joke books? You have to know good literature if you're going to be a writer. My mom says you're just working out your problems with those stupid pencils and the stories about their lives. My mom says . . ."

"Oh, shut up," Emily snapped. "Just because your mother's a psychiatrist and . . ."

"A psychiatric social worker!"

". . . has to pick everyone apart. Maybe I like what I'm doing. Did you ever consider that? I hate reading books. I'd rather write them."

"But you *don't write,*" Carla protested. "You just *tell* them."

"Well, I will write them down—when I'm ready. Maybe I'm planning a whole career of writing for soap operas. Someone has to write them, you know. And how can you say those things don't happen? You changed *your* name, didn't you? Laura to Carla—legally, in court?"

"Well, my mom said I could if it would make me happier with myself. And I did and I am. My insomnia's even gotten better. But that's not the part about your stories that bugs me. It's all the overdramatic stuff—the murders and kidnappings and brain operations are things that just don't happen to ordinary people."

Emily stood up, squinting again to see if she could identify the strange brownish thing over on the island. "Come on, let's go. Maybe we'll find some of those skinny, bright-red starfish you like to look at. I don't want to argue, Carla, really I don't. I wish sometimes I could change my name, too. I'd be Christina or Alexandra. Or maybe Danielle. Do you like Danielle?"

Carla laughed and stood up, too. "Why *do* we argue? It's silly when we like each other so much."

"Oh, *we* don't argue," Emily insisted. "It's only when your mom butts in . . . 'my mom says, my mom says' . . . How come you always talk about your mom and never about your dad?"

Carefully Carla brushed off the seat of her Levi's. "Because he and I are so much alike that he doesn't *influence* me a whole lot. I shouldn't let my mom influence me so much. Even she says—oh, yes, and by the way—I've been meaning to tell you, talking about Mom reminds me that she keeps saying we're getting into a terrible habit of talking all in *italics*. My mom says it's a bad habit, a sign of . . ."

Emily threw one leg over her bicycle and stood poised, ready to pedal off again. "I'm going to *Bolinas* to *explore*. I intend to look for *things*—like deer tracks on Kent Island left from when they swim over at night.

If you want to come, Carla Stiefel or Laura Stiefel or whatever your name is, you'd *better leave your mom behind!*"

Their bikes were chained to a power pole in town and the two girls were wading in the mudflats between the waterfront houses and Kent Island. Spouts of water kept squirting up from the mud as they walked.

"Clams," said Carla. "Maybe we can find someone who will lend us a bucket and shovels so we can dig some."

"Not me," Emily declared, squishing on ahead of Carla. "I'm looking for Japanese glass fishing balls, deer tracks, messages in bottles—or those boots I thought I saw from the highway on the other side. Yes, look, Car-Car, maybe I *did* see boots. Over there in the high grass, near that bent pine tree. Isn't that a pair of waders?"

"It looks like two muddy rocks to me. Really, Emily, we bike miles and miles to see a minus tide and you're only interested in a pair of muddy boots. Well, I'm not! I'm going under the pilings to look for crabs and starfish. And don't call me 'Car-Car.' That's so childish."

Carla said she was going, but she didn't move. Emily turned her back on the island and stood there trying to decide whether to follow her or not. As she was thinking it over, she gazed past Carla, straining for a better look at the narrow mouth of the lagoon. "Maybe we should go over to the mouth and wait," she said. "I've always wanted to be there just when the tide changes—to see the water stop going out and start coming in. I'd like, just once, to see the exact minute it changes. Wouldn't you?"

Carla shook her head. "Not really. Why? If you know it happens, why do you have to see it?"

"Because. Because—because . . ." Emily answered, shifting her gaze from the mouth of the lagoon and fastening it on Carla. For a moment she stared hard at her friend. Then she spoke again. "You know, Car-Car," she said thoughtfully, "you're starting to get bumps."

"I am not. I don't have a bit of acne."

"Not that kind of bumps." Emily laughed. "On your chest. I've never noticed before, but today I can see them right through your t-shirt."

Carla stomped on the mud so hard that it splattered up on both of them. "Really, Emily! *Bumps!* Say *breasts*. When you have to urinate, do you say you're going 'wee-wee'? And, anyway, I am *not* getting *breasts*."

Emily laughed and turned away. "Funny," she mused, pulling on one ponytail, "I'm so much taller. I always thought it would be me first." She didn't say anything more to Carla. She just started picking her way over the mud and small rivers of lagoon water to the island.

On the way, she found an old fossilized-looking nickel and a good piece of twine. She put them both in her pocket. She was curious about the boots, but not really in any hurry. She wasn't going to put on anyone's old pair of boots and go wading in them. She only wanted to look at them, for reasons she couldn't explain and Carla would never understand anyway. Carla, still fuming, had gone in another direction, under the pilings to look for starfish. But Emily didn't care. She liked the slurping sound the mud made as her bare feet sank into it. If she had to come to the lagoon, her favorite occupation there was padding through the mud, scavenging for washed-up junk. On the porch of their house, she had boxes filled with junk she'd collected. She kept meaning to find uses for these things, but mostly they just sat there.

As Emily got closer to the island, she noted with a certain smugness that it *was* a pair of wading boots she'd spotted from all the way across the lagoon. "Funny," she told herself, "that two boots should be washed in together."

She found herself rubbing at her eyes as she squished closer. She was still twenty-five yards away from the grassy place where she'd spotted the waders, but something wasn't right about them. They looked as if they were attached to something. To a man-shaped thing. To something that might have once been a man but was now dead and cold and wet and blown-up like a ghastly brownish balloon—a balloon surrounded by flies.

Moving mechanically, she kept walking closer to the man-shaped dead thing, looking at it and the grass and the waders and at a blue denim bag which seemed to have been washed up nearby. Attached to the blue bag was a shiny golden pen. Or maybe it was a shiny golden pencil. Whatever, it was better to look at than the man-thing. She dropped down on one knee near the bag. As she did, she caught sight of a face. The thing had a face. It was then that the screaming started. Her voice was screaming. "A body! A man! A dead man! Carla. Carla. A dead man's body! A man. A dead man!"

Carla came as fast as she could, but other people came, too. Emily's shrill screams carried far over the water and were heard up and down the main street of Bolinas. A few minutes before, the two girls had been alone in the lagoon, but now others came hurrying there from the town. A lot of curious people were shedding their shoes and wading into the water and mud to see the dead man. Emily heard their feet going splat-squish, but she didn't move. She just knelt there as though she was permanently glued to the spot. She couldn't seem to move anything but her mouth. It was still putting out shrill, hysterical sounds.

Now Carla was behind her shoulder saying something. Despite her own screaming, Emily heard it. "This is more dramatic than your pencil families," Carla said. "I think I'm going to vomit."

Abruptly Emily stopped screaming and closed her mouth. First, she was aware of her own dizziness and then she was conscious of the silence. Not even the birds were shrieking now. A lot of people were standing around—shopkeepers from the town and hippie-type students from the beach—but they were all very quiet. A siren was wailing from the other side of the lagoon. Or maybe it was two sirens, but here, close to the man-shaped body, there wasn't any noise. People were whispering and pointing their fingers at the thing in the waders.

"Are you all right, little girl?" a fat man asked, pulling her to her feet. "Why don't you move back and sit down for a minute? Would you like a mint?" The man had on a suit and a tie with a silver clip. On his feet were muddy socks but no shoes. In his fingers dangled a set of car keys with a monkeyhead key chain. Looking at him made Emily feel like laughing. Hysterically. "Would you like me to give you a ride home?"

Emily shook her head. "I'm okay," she mumbled. But she did move away a few feet and sit down. The wet, cold mud oozed right through the seat of her jeans, but she kept sitting there, wishing Carla would come and sit next to her. Carla was busy, however. She was pressing right in through the crowd, despite her threat of vomiting.

As Emily sat there, some policemen, still wearing their shoes, came running and splashing out to the island. Then their deep policeman-voices began to ask questions of the hushed crowd. Emily was listening to their questions when she suddenly realized that she was holding something in her hand. She looked down frowning as she saw that she was holding a shiny gold pencil. It must be the one she'd seen before attached to the denim bag which was lying near the dead man's boot, but it disturbed her that she didn't even remember picking it up.

Rolling the pencil over and over between her fingers, she stared at it—stared at it until she began to feel as if someone was staring at her. When she looked up, she saw she'd been right. A chunky teen-aged boy was standing a few feet away looking at her. He had curly black hair and was wearing a furry white vest—real fur like a rabbit. He had on faded jeans with a patch on the right knee. The patch said Truck it. Emily stared right back at him until he turned his eyes away. But, every minute or so, Emily would see him look back at her again. He was with another boy, a taller one in an Army shirt. A boy who wore a shiny brass sun-pendant hanging on his chest.

Emily shivered. Then, licking her salty-tasting lips, she looked up past the boys and the rest of the crowd. The body was covered with a blanket now. Nothing showed except the tips of the muddy waders. She raised her eyes higher. Wisps of fog were starting to blow in from the mouth of the lagoon, from over the ocean. She was shivering because it was getting colder. Fingers of mist were rising up from the mudflats. The tide would start coming in soon, the tide and the fog. It was going to be cold bicycling home.

When she looked down again, she saw that the rabbit-vested boy was still watching her, standing closer now as she sat in the mud clutching a shiny pencil that didn't belong to her. She put the pencil in her pocket. Then she heard a policeman asking the rabbit-boy and his friend if they'd seen anything they could report.

"No," he answered in a high-pitched girl's voice. "I just came when that kid screamed. Ask her, why don't you?"

Emily rubbed at her eyes. That wasn't a rabbit-vested boy. It was a girl. "What's wrong with me?" Emily asked herself. "Am I so mixed up I can't tell a boy from a girl anymore?"

The policeman bent down in the mud next to her. He had shaggy eyebrows that grew in one straight line across the top of his nose. Emily could see the water soaking over the tops of his shoes. "Well, young lady, would you like to make a statement for me?"

"Lawrence won't believe me," she told the policeman.

"Who's Lawrence?"

"My brother. Say . . . I just thought of something . . ."

"What?" asked the policeman.

"What's yellow and goes click-click?"

The policeman stood up again. "A ball-point banana," he muttered. "I have kids, too. Now, isn't there anyone here who can give me an intelligent statement?"

# 3

"Two local girls found a dead man in the lagoon today," Nettie declared as Emily opened the door of the Mendle house. "I just heard that on the radio. I was listening while I tried out your mother's bread recipe—the wheat bread recipe she had tacked up over the stove. The police think he'd been murdered."

Emily was cold and numb after biking back from Bolinas in the wind and fog. She went right to the stove and put her hands on top where the two pilot lights warmed up the enamel. Her fingers were so icy that the warm stove felt as if it were burning her, so she had to pull her hands away and rub them together. "Is Lawrence home?" she asked.

"In his room," Nettie said with a nod. "Finishing up work on the screen that goes behind his science fair project." As she talked she kept on kneading the lumpy brown mound of dough against the table. "Did you hear what I said about the dead man, Emily? His name was Willard Conners. He lived alone on the lagoon in Bolinas—second house from the end. They think he drowned, and his house had been robbed, too. You know, your mother's recipe doesn't use as much flour as mine. You were over near Bolinas, weren't you? Did you see anything?"

"Lawrence," Emily called, turning her back on Nettie. "Law-rence! Law-rence! Law-rence!"

To her great surprise, he came immediately. With heavy thudding steps he ran to find her. "What?" he asked. "What is it? Are you all right, Em? You were bellowing like someone was trying to kill you."

*"Someone killed him,"* Emily said.

"Who?" Lawrence asked, already beginning to back away. He had seen her standing there, looking fine, and he no longer seemed quite so concerned about her.

Emily lunged forward and grabbed him by the front of his baggy sweatshirt. "Don't go," she pleaded. "There was this dead man in the lagoon. All swollen, and I found him because of the waders. Carla says things like that don't happen to *real* people—only to pencil families. But he was so dead, Lawrence, so dead that his eyes were gone from the eyeballs."

Lawrence frowned. "Come on, Em. You're playing games again."

"No, I'm not. I swear I'm not."

"Are you serious? Look at me. You're not joking? This isn't your idea of a weird joke?"

"No, it really happened. Ask Nettie. She heard about it on the radio."

"*You* found that body?" Nettie asked incredulously. "You and Carla were the two girls?"

"You are serious!" Lawrence said. "You actually found a corpse? God, that must have been awful. A real shock. Come over here, Em. Sit down, will you?"

Emily could feel a silly grin spreading across her face, but she didn't care. For once, Lawrence was actually interested in listening to what she had to say. He and Nettie wrapped her in a blanket, lit a fire, and began to ply her with questions. Nettie brought a glass of warm milk with honey in it for her to drink, and Lawrence sat down on the couch next to her. Nettie asked most of the questions, but Lawrence was listening. He was paying attention to every word she spoke.

It didn't take long for Emily to start feeling rather happy. Wrapped up and sipping warm milk, she sat next to her brother and told him of her grisly find. After a while, she began supplying all kinds of minute details about the body, the lagoon, and the crowd that had assembled—details she'd hardly been conscious of seeing at the time.

Nettie kept pounding at the wheat bread dough as she listened and prodded Emily for more information. "His name was Willard Conners," she said. "The radio announced that. But why didn't they give your name and Carla's when you two did the finding, instead of saying 'two local girls'? Why didn't you give them your names?"

"We did," Emily replied, snuggling down into the blanket. "At least Carla did. She gave them to the policeman—the one with the eyebrows that grew straight across. First the rabbit-vested boy, I mean, girl said to ask me and he did. But he—the policeman—complained about what I was saying and asked if there wasn't someone intelligent around to answer him, so that's when Carla came over and told him everything."

"Thank goodness for Carla," Lawrence said, getting up from the couch and going over to the desk. Emily was disappointed to see him move farther away, but she was relieved to see he hadn't stopped looking at her to look back into his microscope. He was frowning and scratching his head—staring at Emily as though he was about to say something important.

"Maybe the police will come here and ring our bell, wanting to ask you more questions," Nettie said. "Do they know your address? It would be very exciting to have them come by. You really had quite an experience, Em. How come something like that happens to *you*? Things almost happen to me, but nothing really happens. That's the story of my life. Nothing exciting happens to me any more. Do you think it's too late?"

Before Emily could begin to answer Nettie, Lawrence spoke. His voice was very stern. "Listen, Emily, I'm glad you told us about the body, but I don't want you to say a word to Dad and Ma when they call. You mustn't upset them and ruin their week."

Still wrapped in the blanket, Emily stood up and began taking mincing little steps toward her brother. "Well, maybe I *want* to upset them. Did that ever occur to you? It was *upsetting* to find a corpse. I *feel* upset. Do you hear me, Lawrence?"

Lawrence nodded. "I hear you, but you are still going to do as I say. I am older and sometimes, like it or not, you have to listen to me and do exactly what I tell you to do!" As soon as he had finished speaking, he picked up a pencil and started taking notes on a yellow tablet. Apparently he'd said all he was going to say and listened all he was going to listen. A corpse in the lagoon was worth about twenty-three minutes of his time and no more, even if his own sister had discovered it. He'd already lost interest and gone back to scribbling some of his endless notes. Was that one of her pencils in his hand? Emily squinted. She thought it looked suspiciously like Mrs. Ticonderoga. Had Lawrence stolen it from her room?

"Do you hear me, Lawrence?" Emily repeated, moving a little closer. *"I am upset."*

"Yes," he muttered, still writing on that tablet. "But you're still not going to tell Dad and Ma. If you're upset, talk to me or to Nettie. That's what we're here for. But not to them. Absolutely not to them. Now let's change the subject. Did you bring me any water samples from the lagoon? This is my last night to work, you know, because I'm submitting my plankton project in the morning."

Emily gnashed her teeth together. She wanted to stamp her foot, but she couldn't because she was still wrapped in folds of blanket. "I find a dead man in the lagoon and all you can ask is if I brought you water samples for your science project. You are the most awful, inconsiderate, mean, ugly, thoughtless, cruel . . ."

As she was warming up to carry on a real tirade, the phone rang. She hopped forward, hoping to get to it before her brother, hoping it was her parents on the line. But Lawrence picked it up first. He said hello, listened for a moment, and then he said, "No, this is not Western Union. You have to dial the area code before the number. Dial 800 first." When he had finished explaining about the area code, he banged down the phone. Then, before Emily could start yelling at him again, he simply stood up and walked out of the room.

Emily was still standing there with her mouth open, only there wasn't anyone to shout at. She couldn't believe it. Even finding a dead man wasn't important or outrageous enough to make him really notice her. Maybe if she threw up all over the floor, he'd come running back and take her more seriously. But she didn't feel like throwing up. She felt like crying, and yet she wasn't going to cry. She never gave Lawrence the satisfaction of thinking he could make her cry.

At least Nettie cared. That was some consolation. "Tell me more, hon," she urged. "Any little thing you remember. It's quite a story really—even better than your pencil-people stories. Maybe you can sort of work it in somewhere. Come on now—tell me more."

"Later," Emily promised, letting the blanket fall to the floor in a heap. "Not any more now. It makes me all shivery to keep thinking about it. So, can I help with the bread for a while? Or can I help with dinner?"

Nettie didn't give up that easily. She agreed to let Emily help with the bread and with dinner, but as they worked she kept right on asking questions.

"How do you think he died? Did he really drown or was he shot? Did you see any bullet holes?" she asked as she began braiding some of the dough into a long loaf. "Why don't you braid yours into a ring, hon?"

Choosing to ignore the matter of bullet holes, Emily talked to Nettie about the bread. "Braiding is boring. I'm going to make a bread man. That's what I do with Ma when she's here."

Then Emily rolled a ball of dough for the head, another for the body, and long thin sausage-shaped rolls for the arms and legs. She gave her bread man raisin eyes and buttons. But all the time she was working with the dough, she was brooding about Lawrence. Brooding that he had so quickly lost interest in her and in what had happened to her at the lagoon. He didn't even think it was important enough to tell Ma and Dad. Lawrence was much more concerned about them than about her.

"Do something else outrageous," she muttered to herself as she shaped the feet of her bread man.

"What?" asked Nettie. "Did you say something? Do you think the police will come tonight?"

"Not to talk to me, Netts. If they come, it will be to see you. About all the flowers missing from the gardens around here. Like the purple ones in your hair."

Now it was Nettie's turn to change the subject. "If you're finished with your little man, put him over by the fireplace. The heat will make the dough rise faster. Would you like to taste my lamb stew and see if there's anything it needs? You're so creative about cooking. I tried to be a creative cook once, and I almost won a bread-baking contest. But they disqualified me for baking three dyed eggs into the top of the loaf. The judges said no decorations were allowed—even if it was Easter week. But look at you, Emily, look what you've done with a lump of dough."

Smiling broadly, Emily nodded. She could see through Nettie's flattery. Nettie wanted her to take over the work of finishing up and serving dinner. But she didn't really mind. She *was* rather good in the kitchen and Nettie wasn't. Nettie was good at sewing and talking, but there wasn't much else she ever seemed to care about.

Tonight, Emily noticed, Nettie was already wearing a finished muu-muu made out of the cloth she'd been pinning a pattern to just the night before. It had yellow and green pineapples on it and a ruffle over the shoulders. Nettie's red-dyed hair was piled up on her head with a bunch of purple flowers wilting in the middle of the whole arrangement. Nettie was drinking something out of a glass as she talked to Emily. It looked like ice water, but it could have been some of the vodka from the bottles Nettie kept hidden in the back pantry.

"What do you need so many Hawaiian dresses for?" Emliy asked, putting her bread man near the fire.

"I don't. I make them and sell them to my neighbors on Amsterdam Street in the city. I pick up extra money that way. Once, down South, I had a chance to go into the business—the rag business, it's called. I almost did, but the boss's son—my boyfriend—got killed in the war, and that ended that."

"What war?" Emily asked.

Nettie took a big swallow out of her glass. "I don't remember."

"Well then, tell me . . . how can you *sell* those dresses if you wear them all first?"

"Just one or two times to break them in a little," Nettie conceded. "Are you going to taste the stew now, while I freshen up and call Lawrence? I do want to look my best if the police should come by tonight."

Emily's head was filled with pictures of Nettie's lost boyfriend and of all the ladies on hilly Amsterdam Street walking up and down in Nettie's flowered muumuus. Filling her head with these pictures helped empty out the memory of what she had seen at the lagoon. But, still, she wasn't daydreaming so much that she couldn't hear the words "Lawrence" and "stew."

"Something outrageous," she mumbled to herself. "Yes, you go wash up, Netts. I'll take care of the stew."

And she did. First she took a pot holder and a big wooden spoon. Then, feeling extraordinarily capable, she decided to doctor up the stew and hear the final arguments in Mrs. Ticonderoga's murder trial at the same time. Maybe playing with pencils *was* childish, as Carla said, but it was better than thinking about a dead body.

So, with the pencil families packing the windowsill gallery above the stove, she presided over the court as Judge Mendle, stirring the stew as she listened. She had considered letting the new gold pencil—the one from the lagoon—act as judge, but had abandoned that idea, feeling that she knew the families' problems better.

"But your honor," Mrs. Ticonderoga pleaded emotionally. "I didn't mean to shoot my brother Sam Campus. It was an accident. Oh, yes, we argued. Yes, we did.

Over our company, the Aloha Hawaiian Muu-Muu Corporation. You see, I was the designer, but he was so busy with the company books, and he never gave me credit for anything. Oh, yes, I hated him so badly I would have strangled him with my bare hands, but *not* shot him. Not my own brother. The gun went off accidentally while I was cleaning it. And he just happened to be three feet away at the time."

As Emily considered Mrs. Ticonderoga's defense, she worked on the lamb stew, adding a little bit of this and that, doctoring it up until it looked beautiful. Now Nettie's reddish-brown stew was the loveliest shade of dark, rich satiny-brown. It would be just perfect for Lawrence.

# 4

"What did you do, Em? What ever did you put in it?" Nettie asked as they sat down to dinner. "That color is absolutely mouth-watering."

"Shoepolish," Emily said, watching Lawrence slide into his chair and start spooning a huge helping onto his earthenware plate.

Nettie laughed and scooped out a helping for herself. "What an imaginative girl you are. One in a million. Lawrence may be book-smart, but he can't hold a candle to you! Shoepolish! I was thinking of poisoning one of my boyfriends once—not with shoepolish but with snail bait. That was when I was down South where the snails were really something terrible. Imagine—telling us you put shoepolish in the stew."

"I put *shoepolish* in it," Emily shouted at Lawrence who was only two feet away from her. "Do you like the stew, Lawrence? I flavored it with shoepolish!"

"Very funny," Lawrence answered, his mouth bulging with stew. "You're so immature. Even little Willy McHenry who's only nine is smarter than you." Then Lawrence looked down and started filling in blank spaces on the crossword puzzle he'd brought to the table.

With a sigh, Emily helped herself to a large portion of salad and a small helping of stew. She felt smug as she watched Lawrence gobble up his dinner. She almost forgave him for working on the puzzle when she saw how much stew he was shoveling into his mouth. She was watching him reach out for a third helping when the doorbell rang.

"I'll get it," she volunteered, bouncing up from the table.

She ran to the front door, opened it, and found herself looking up at a tall boy of about eighteen or nineteen. He had on an old Army shirt and muddy jeans. Around his neck hung a large, brass sun-shaped pendant.

"I'm selling magazines," the tall boy said, pointing to a clipboard dangling from one hand. "To work my way through college. Can I interest you in a subscription to something?"

"What do you really want?" Emily asked, already beginning to close the door partway. "You're not selling magazines."

"Oh, I am," the boy insisted. "Really I am, but I'm in bad shape. You see, I lost my pencil. Someone stole it, and I can't fill in my magazine contracts without a pencil. If I could just borrow one from you—just to use on this street. I'd return it. I promise. But I need a special kind of pencil, you see. Something classy looking. Shiny maybe—if you have something like that. It impresses the customers, you see."

Emily stared up at this boy. He had dark-blue eyes which were fringed with stubby brown lashes. Looking at him made her stomach feel funny. She'd seen this boy once before today, at the lagoon, when she'd been sitting in the mud rolling the shiny gold pencil between her fingers. The pencil? Was it still in her back pocket? She patted behind her to see. Yes, it was. The boy seemed to see what she was doing and moved one foot into the doorway. As he did so, Emily lunged forward and fastened the door chain.

"Oh, please," the boy pleaded through the narrow, chained opening of the doorway. "Just lend me a pencil. I'll return it. I'll even give you a tip, if you want. Some money to spend on candy."

"I can't eat candy," Emily said. "I have braces."

"Why, yes, you do. I used to have braces. Do your friends call you Metalmouth or Tinselteeth? Mine did. Do they tell you you have railroad tracks in your mouth?"

"Sometimes."

"Well, you can spend the money on something else, then. And I'll return your pencil. Really I will. You wouldn't want to be responsible for keeping me from getting into college, would you? Come on, girl. I bet you have a pencil right in your pocket, don't you?"

Emily swallowed hard. "No," she lied, pushing at the door in an attempt to close it all the way. But she couldn't because the tall boy on the other side still had his foot wedged in it, and he was pushing against it, too.

While Emily was struggling with the door, Nettie called out to her. "Who is it, hon?"

"A boy selling magazines," she answered.

"Don't let him in, for heaven's sake."

"I won't," Emily promised.

"Oh, come on," begged the boy, "unchain the door. I'm not here to make trouble for anyone. Say, maybe if I can't have a pencil, you'll do something else for me. How about a glass of water? Can't I come in and get a drink, at least?"

"No," said a deep voice from behind Emily's left shoulder.

Still leaning against the door, she managed to turn her head far enough to grin at Lawrence. She was pleased he'd come to help her out.

Standing very straight, he stepped right up to the open crack. Emily could see that he was doing his best to seem as tall and as old as the boy on the other side of the door. "Now what's this all about?" he asked. "Who are you and what do you want? Why are you picking on a little kid? We don't want any magazines. Didn't she tell you that? I may just have to call the police . . ."

Lawrence's threatening words made Emily begin to feel quite brave. "I've seen him before," she told her brother.

"No, you haven't," said the boy.

"Oh, yes," Emily insisted. "Today at the lagoon where the dead man was."

"Not me. That wasn't me!" the boy protested.

"Yes, it was. And you were there with a girl—a boyish-looking girl wearing a rabbity vest."

As she was saying "rabbity vest" the boy suddenly withdrew his foot and let go of the door. It slammed shut. Emily quickly turned the bolt.

Lawrence was standing next to her with a puzzled look on his face. "What was that all about? Have you really seen him before?"

"I think so," Emily answered, patting her back pocket to make sure the gold pencil was still there.

"But you don't actually *know* him."

"No . . ." Emily conceded.

"Then he's really a stranger, isn't he?"

"Well . . . yes."

Lawrence made a face. "Then you oughtn't to rush and open the front door when you don't even know who's standing outside. Especially when Ma and Dad aren't home. Next time the bell rings at night, you'd better let me answer it."

Emily smiled. "All right. Sure," she agreed. Having Lawrence so concerned almost made her forget how strange it was to have the boy from the lagoon show up at her front door.

"Come on," said Lawrence. "Let's finish dinner so I can get back to work."

"I'm glad you had enough sense not to let that boy in," Nettie said as they came back into the living room. "You can't be too careful nowadays. Especially with the robberies around here. And now a murder, too. A murderer who wiped out poor Willard Conners."

Lawrence didn't return to the table. As Emily slid back into her seat, she saw that he was in the kitchen, rummaging through a drawer, tossing out screwdrivers, aspirin bottles, balls of twine, and old keys. He was muttering to himself, too. He was already preoccupied again, Emily noticed. In a few seconds, he'd forgotten about her and the stranger at the door.

After pawing through the drawer for a while, he turned around and faced Emily. The vague look on his face disappeared as his eyes began to focus accusingly on her. "All right. Where's the shoepolish?" he yelled. "I know I left it right here."

Emily smiled. "In the stew," she answered, hoping Lawrence wouldn't turn around and see the tiny bottles of food coloring she'd left on the stove. "You ate it. How else was I supposed to get that pretty brown color?"

"Oh, forget it. I'll find it myself. Or I'll show up at the fair tomorrow without my shoes polished." Without giving one more glance in Emily's direction, he flopped into the big chair by the piano, picked up a thick green book and started to read.

Feeling full of hate for Lawrence, who could be so kind one moment and so dreadful the next, Emily helped Nettie clear the table and put the now-risen bread dough into the oven. They left the dishes for Lawrence. It was *his* night, and Emily was not about to do him any favors.

When Nettie went to take a shower, Emily hung around to keep an eye on the baking bread. She sat on the floor in front of the little black-and-white TV, but she wasn't really watching it, even though the volume was turned up loud in an attempt to annoy Lawrence. She was waiting for him to get up to do the dishes. For him to find the shoepolish bottle she'd retrieved from the garbage can and placed on the stove after she put the food coloring away.

She kept thinking about the pencil in her back pocket and about the Army-shirted boy who had rung their bell. It was a weird coincidence to have him showing up here. Maybe she should have given him the pencil, just to get rid of it. Maybe she should have given it to the policeman with the bushy eyebrows. What was she going to do with it? If she added it to her pencil families, it would just be one of the orphans—one of the pencils with no family name on it.

Pulling it out of her pocket, she looked at it for the first time since she'd left the lagoon. It wasn't an important pencil, she told herself. It wasn't evidence. It didn't say Willard Conners. It just said Blythe Queen. That didn't mean anything. It was a brand name, like on her other pencils, a brand name like Ticonderoga or Dixon.

Looking at it made her feel chilly. She really hadn't gotten all warmed-up since she'd been back. She crawled over and sat on the floor next to the oven, peering in through its glass window. It was warmer there. As she looked in, she could see Nettie's braided loaf puffing up and her wheat bread man, too.

Something about the little man caught her attention. She leaned her head sideways and stared at it for a minute. Then she called to her brother. "Lawrence, come here quick. Come see my bread man. He's turned all brownish and he's breathing here in the oven. I can see the dough on his chest going up and down as he bakes. Come here, quick!"

Lawrence didn't answer. He was sitting at the desk, surrounded by stacks of white paper, furiously retyping pages of his already-typed project.

"The man's breathing," Emily mused, knowing that nothing she said would interest Lawrence enough to come and look. So she sat alone by the oven watching her wheat bread man bake. In and out his chest went as he breathed. Then, suddenly, despite the heat from the oven, Emily shivered. Willard Conners wasn't breathing. He was dead.

# 5

"Go on, Lawrence," Emily insisted. "I'm okay here by myself. You get Ted and David, and I'll meet you at the bus stop at 10:30."

"Do you have to come? Why don't you go to Carla's house for the day? You're going to hate it. You'll be bored and complain."

Emily grinned. "Your shoelace is untied," she said. "And besides, Ma said on the phone last night that you *had* to take me since Nettie's gone to San Rafael for the day. Anyway, you owe it to me because I did what you said and didn't tell about finding the dead body."

Lawrence picked up the large cardboard carton that held his science project for the fair in the city. "All right. But if you're not there at 10:30—at the bus stop—we're going to leave without you."

As Lawrence started toward the door, Emily remembered something. "Hey . . ." she said.

"What?"

"Well . . . before you go, there's one more thing. Maybe I shouldn't even say anything. Maybe . . ."

"Try me."

"Well, a few minutes ago, I thought I heard strange

noises out in back of the house. It made me feel shivery. Like someone was coming after me—the someone who killed Mr. Conners and who might be looking for me, thinking I know something special."

"You're a dimwit. You know that?"

"No, I heard something out back. You must believe me!"

Lawrence juggled the heavy carton as he opened the front door. "Okay, okay. I'll take a quick look on my way out, if it will make you feel better. But you'd better move your tail and dress so you'll be at the bus stop on time. This fair is very important to me, Emily, and I'm not going to let you louse things up."

Emily came out on the deck and stood there in her red flannel bathrobe while Lawrence begrudgingly circled the house. "There's no one here," he assured her as he came around from behind the garage. "It must have been your overactive imagination again. Now go get dressed, will you?"

As soon as Lawrence had disappeared around the bend in the road, Emily went inside, closed the door, threw off her robe, and got to work. She had a lot to do before 10:30 to fix up the surprise for Lawrence. This was going to be a memorable day for him. She was planning to make full use of what he called her "overactive imagination" so he would not be able to overlook her today.

With great care, she assembled her outfit—even borrowing one or two little things from Nettie. As she was pulling on her socks though, she began to think she heard some kind of crackling noise on the hillside near the house.

Carefully edging up to one of the back windows, she looked out. Maybe she was hearing things this morning. Or maybe it was Lawrence and his friends sneaking back to play a prank on her. She never should have told him she heard noises outside the house. Although she peered around in every possible direction, she didn't see anyone or anything suspicious. So, after a few minutes, she went back to finish her work.

As soon as she was through, she ran to her parents' room where she examined herself in the full-length mirror, turning from side to side until she was entirely satisfied. Then, feeling that there was no way to improve her appearance further, she grabbed her knapsack, ran out of the house and down the hill, making it to the bus stop at exactly 10:29. The boys were waiting for her. So was the green and white bus.

"Do you think you could have cut it any closer?" Lawrence growled as he and his friends followed Emily up the steps into the bus.

"I got here, didn't I?" she asked brightly.

"Yeah, yeah—I guess so. Now look, Emily, I want you to just sit down right here, next to me, and be quiet.

I don't want you to make a pest of yourself, understand?"

"I don't have to be quiet," Emily insisted as she slid into the seat. "Ma said you should be *nice,* remember?" Then, ignoring Lawrence, she stood up halfway out of her seat and leaned forward, so she had her head between the heads of his two friends, David Tock and Ted Sweeny. "I'm not a pest, am I?" she asked, looking from one to the other. David was Lawrence's best friend, and he was always good to Emily. She liked him, especially when he laughed. He had a wonderful froggy laugh. The other boy, Ted Sweeny, was interested in science like Lawrence. He never talked very much. Emily thought it might have been because of his stutter. If he didn't talk a lot, he wouldn't embarrass himself by stumbling over his words.

David Tock looked at Emily as she leaned forward next to him. Reaching out, he pulled gently on one of her ponytails. "You're okay, kid," he said. "Always good for a laugh."

Emily didn't sit back in her seat. She kept hoping Lawrence would get annoyed enough to yank her down. But he wasn't paying any attention. He had the carton on his lap and on top of it he had a tablet which was being used for taking down some new notes.

"Hey, David," Emily said. "What's black and white and has fuzz inside?"

"A rattlesnake that swallowed a caterpillar?" David asked, pushing his long sandy hair out of his face and grinning at her.

"No, silly." Emily giggled. "A police car!"

"A police car," David repeated, laughing in his deep froggy way. "Did you hear that, Ted? Black and white with fuzz inside—a police car. Was that the kind of police car that came to the lagoon yesterday when you found the dead man?"

Emily nodded.

"W-weren't you scared?" Ted asked.

"No," Emily lied. "I'm used to things like that. They happen all the time to my pencil families."

"Pencil families?" David asked. "What are pencil families?"

He really seemed to want to know, so all the rest of the way into San Francisco, Emily told him and told Ted about the Dixons, the Ticonderogas, the Choices, the Eberhard-Fabers, and the pencil orphans. She also told them about the Queen who had moved into their neighborhood. A blythe Queen without a throne, who was having a terrible time adjusting to being a commoner and putting up with life in pencil suburbia. "The real problem," Emily confided as they were crossing the Golden Gate Bridge, "is that Mrs. Choice is nervous because Mr. Choice—her new husband—seems to be paying too much attention to the Queen. He's even stopped calling her 'Your majesty' and started calling her 'Queenie.' "

Lawrence's friends laughed uproariously, so uproariously that Emily kept right on describing the perils of her pencils. Soon the two boys were laughing so loud that Lawrence looked up from his scribbling. "Shut up, Emily," he muttered. "You're making a scene."

Emily dropped back into her seat, smiling smugly. "Oh, really?" she said.

When the four of them arrived at the Academy of Sciences, Lawrence put away his tablet and took charge. First he checked in at the main desk and found out where he was supposed to set up his plankton exhibit and paper. Emily, David, and Ted stood around as Lawrence patiently readjusted the sequence of his scientific drawings and thumbed through his eighty-four-page paper on *Plankton of the Bolinas Estuary*. Lawrence was quite disturbed when he discovered that page 67 was somehow missing from the report.

"Well, there's nothing you can do about it now," David said. "Why don't you bring it in tomorrow? The judging's not 'til Friday night."

Glumly, Lawrence agreed. Then he and the others began to wander up and down the aisles looking at exhibits that other students had submitted. Emily tagged along behind the boys. She was vaguely intrigued by the cigarette-smoking machine and by a beautiful exhibit of homegrown multicolored crystals, but nothing really seemed as good to her as her brother's elaborate presentation. After a while, she began to feel bored and draggy.

"What's wrinkled and goes slam-slam-slam-slam?" she whispered, catching hold of David's arm.

"What?" he whispered back.

"A four-door prune," Emily said. "Say, do you know you still have milk on your mouth from breakfast—but not quite as much of a moustache as Lawrence? And why do you always wear your shirts unbuttoned halfway down your chest?"

"Listen, Emily baby," David said, doing a terrible gangster imitation, "that's cool. And I like to be cool, baby."

Emily laughed. "If you had hair on your chest, you'd be even cooler. Or would you be warmer?" As David chuckled at her, she twisted her hands together. Then she spoke again. "Say, there's something else I've always wanted to ask you."

"Shoot."

"Why do you have number 432 inked on your sneakers?"

"My locker number, sweetie. So no one will rip 'em

off. You can't trust anyone these days—not even in Stinson or Bolinas. And now there's a murderer loose, isn't there?"

"Yes—and I'm worried," Emily told David. "Get Ted and come over here where we can talk.

"I may even be in danger," Emily confided to the two boys after she had managed to get them onto a corner bench with her. "That murderer might be after me, you know. Thinking I know something about who robbed and killed Mr. Conners. About who hit him on the head and dumped him into the lagoon. This morning, I thought someone was outside our house, looking in at me, and now I keep getting the feeling that I'm being followed."

"By who?" Ted asked, looking all around.

Emily shrugged. "Suspicious people. A tall boy in an Army shirt, maybe. This is serious, you guys. Really serious."

"Okay, kid," David agreed. "We'll help you out. We'll be on the lookout for suspicious characters, especially ones in Army shirts. Hey, there's one—over by Lawrence's exhibit. Is that him?"

"No, that's just some old man," Emily said. "And don't tease me. I'm serious. *Deadly* serious. Strange things *have* been happening. People staring at me at the lagoon. Strangers ringing our doorbell. Now, look around here. Strange people are staring at me. It's as if *everyone* was staring at me."

David grinned. "Well, if people *are* staring at you, it might—it might just happen to be related to the way you're dressed."

"The way I'm dressed?" Emily asked innocently.

"Yes, Emily Mendle, you're probably the only ten-year-old girl here wearing a knapsack, one red sock, one green-striped sock, one sneaker, one muddy hiking boot, orange lipstick, purple eyeshadow, and fingernails so long they look like claws."

Emily laughed. "Not bad, huh? I'm a rather creative person, you see. Like the pencil Queen. This is the way she dressed, you know, to attract the attention of Mr. Alexander Choice. Only she wore one glass slipper and one patent-leather boot. What about you, Ted? Do you like the way I look?"

Ted scratched his head. "D-didn't want to hurt your feelings, but I couldn't decide whether you looked like a c-clown or a whore."

"A whore," Emily replied with dignity. "I must be a whore, even though I don't know what that means exactly, because I'm certainly not a clown. Especially since I have to worry so about being followed by suspicious characters. It's *not* a laughing matter, you know."

The boys responded to her pronouncement with

howls of laughter. Then they dragged Emily to her feet so they could rejoin Lawrence and at least pretend to be interested in what was absorbing him. They wandered through several more aisles of exhibits, and it was well past lunchtime when they finally convinced Lawrence that it was time to visit the coffee shop.

As they headed in that direction, Emily was still busy having Ted and David check out every person in an Army shirt. They were still laughing at her, when she tripped down the stairs that led to the coffee shop. Because it was awkward walking with one boot and one sneaker, she suddenly pitched forward and went rolling down, until she managed to catch hold of the bannister and stop herself.

"Come on. Get up," Lawrence urged. "You're blocking the stairway."

Emily didn't budge. She tried moving the ankle which was above the sneakered foot. It had little twinges of pain shooting through it. She tried to twist it back and forth.

"Get up," Lawrence said again. "You're okay."

"Here, I'll h-help," Ted volunteered, reaching down and pulling her to her feet.

"Ohh," she moaned. It did hurt. Not a whole lot, but it hurt. Besides, her legs were tired from all the walking on the cold, hard floors of the museum building. Or maybe they hurt from rocking back and forth in uneven shoes. Also, her shoulders were aching from carrying the heavy knapsack.

"Come on, Ted," David suggested. "The kid needs help. She's really loused up that ankle."

To Emily's delight, Lawrence's two friends took charge of her. For the rest of the day, one or both of them helped her everywhere. Sometimes they made a seat with their arms for her to sit on, and sometimes they carried her knapsack and let her lean on their shoulders. Emily accepted every bit of solicitous help she was offered. Occasionally she would remember to wince in pain, but she never forgot to keep telling the boys how appreciative she was.

As this was all going on, she was watching Lawrence to see how he was reacting. It was hard to tell. He'd never said a word about her outfit or her makeup. Maybe he hadn't even noticed.

Most of the lipstick had come off on the hotdog bun at lunch, and the eyeshadow was giving her some problems, too. Her eyes kept watering, and the edges of her fists were turning a greasy purple from rubbing at them. If Lawrence was oblivious to the outfit and makeup, he didn't seem to be able to overlook the injured ankle, especially since his friends were carrying her around and all but ignoring the science exhibits that Lawrence had brought them to the city to see. Was he jealous of Emily? She couldn't tell since he didn't say much of anything. His lips were pressed tightly together though, and he was carrying his shoulders in a funny, stiff way. Then about 2:30, abruptly, he said, "Let's go home."

"Oh, no," Emily protested. "David promised he'd take me to the aquarium area to see the snakes and alligators."

"I said we're going home, Emily," Lawrence told her.

And they did. All the way back on the bus, Emily chatted with David and Ted. This time she didn't bother to sit with Lawrence. She sat alone—with her foot propped up, on the seat in front of Lawrence's friends—while he sat across the aisle, staring out the window and, as far as Emily could tell, seeing nothing. Was he mad at her? Very very mad? He always yelled when he was mad at her, but today he was alarmingly quiet. Maybe he wasn't even thinking of her. Maybe it was the missing page of his science project that was bugging him.

Emily kept on chattering with the boys, but she never really looked away from her brother. She told Ted and David a few more elephant jokes and how annoyed she was with all the calls coming in for Western Union. "I'm going to start getting back at those people," she declared. "But I don't know exactly how . . ."

After a while, she even consented to let the boys peek into her knapsack to see what was there. Her pencil families. All of them. Even Queenie and the orphans.

"I thought they'd enjoy a day in the city," Emily explained in a much-too-loud voice, hoping Lawrence would look up. He didn't, but David and Ted peered into the bag and roared with laughter.

"Tell me," David asked between deep croaks of laughter, "is the pointed end the head or the feet of a pencil person?"

"The head, of course," Emily answered. "They need the erasers to stand on—sort of like rubber-soled shoes."

Again the boys laughed, but this time David called out to Lawrence. "Your sister is really something," he said.

Lawrence looked up with a mean, frowning face. "My sister is an intolerable, spoiled, loudmouth brat."

David nodded. "Yes . . . yes, you're right—but that's part of her charm."

"Do you need any help getting up the hill to your house?" David asked as they got off the bus at Stinson Beach.

"Well, maybe," Emily said hesitantly. "And then at the house, you can have some of my homemade root beer. I make very good root beer—from a kit. Just ask Lawrence—he loves it."

"Not today," Lawrence snapped. "I don't want anyone over today. And besides, she doesn't need help!"

Emily made a face. "Well . . . thanks," she said,

pulling her pencil-filled knapsack onto her shoulders. "I guess I can make it by myself, and I'll give you my root beer another day, all right? If my ankle hurts, Lawrence will help. Or if he won't, I'll just hop."

Lawrence didn't even say goodbye to his friends. He didn't volunteer to help Emily either. Instead, he stalked on ahead of her up the hill from the bus stop without a word. Emily hopped behind him for a few hundred yards, but he was gaining ground too fast, and she was beginning to worry that he might get home first and lock her out of the house. So she tried walking, remembering to keep a little bit of a limp. When that didn't quite do it, she stopped limping altogether and started a little light-footed jog that made the knapsack full of pencils bounce against her shoulders.

By the time Lawrence turned into their street, Emily was only a few steps behind. She noticed the door of their house at the same time he did. It was standing open. Wide open. Lawrence began to run. So did she. Together they thudded up the front steps and into the house.

It was chaos. Things were thrown everywhere. Cans of food emptied from kitchen cabinets, pillows thrown off the couch, chairs overturned, drawers hanging open.

"We've been robbed!" Lawrence said. "We've been robbed."

# 6

"It must have been Nettie," Emily insisted. "Sick with a migraine. She probably threw everything around looking for her pill bottle."

"I don't think so," Lawrence answered grimly.

"Nettie! Nettie! Netts!" Emily called out. There was no answer. "I guess she's not back yet. We *have* been robbed. I'm scared."

"Well, you go out on the deck and stay there while I search the house," Lawrence told her.

"Why can't I come?" she asked.

"Because I'm trying to look after you—even if you are a pain. Now stay outside, will you, while I take a look?"

"No," Emily insisted, grabbing hold of the back pocket of his jeans. "Where you go, I go."

He shrugged. "Then come. But stick your hands in your own pockets, will you?"

Lawrence went from room to room closely followed by Emily, who was very relieved to find that he didn't seem to be furious with her any more. They looked everywhere, but they found no signs of burglars still lurking in the house. What they did find was more mess and confusion. In the bedrooms, the dresser drawers had been opened and their contents scattered. Mattresses were pulled off the beds. Laundry bags had been emptied of their mounds of dirty, wrinkled clothes. Even Nettie's yards of Hawaiian fabric had been unrolled and left dragging along the floor.

"You're right," Emily whispered. "Real burglars went through the house. All through it. This is one more creepy thing . . ."

Lawrence didn't say anything to her. He just kept walking back through every room mumbling to himself. "My microscope is here, the kitchen radio, the binoculars, Dad's Instamatic. Ma doesn't have any jewelry that isn't made of shells or beads—and it looks like it's all here, anyway. Nettie's vodka is still in the back pantry and the typewriter is on the desk. And all our clothes and things seem to be here . . ."

Emily shook her head. "No, something of mine is missing."

"What?"

"My pewter sand dollar. The one on the thong that Daddy gave me for my birthday."

"Are you sure?" Lawrence asked.

"Sure I'm sure."

Lawrence scratched his head. "You probably left it at Carla's house or lost it somewhere. Why would burglars leave everything else and take that?"

"I don't know," Emily said. "I don't know. It's all creepy—just like I told you."

The expression on Lawrence's face showed his total lack of concern about Emily's loss. "What else haven't we checked out?" he asked.

"What about the silverware?" Emily suggested, standing very close to Lawrence and looking up into his face.

He patted her on the shoulder, making her feel very important. "That's good thinking, Em. Go look."

"I already did," she answered with a proud smile. "It's still here—dumped on the floor in the hall closet. I didn't count, but it doesn't look like anything's missing."

Lawrence gnashed his teeth together. "Well, if you already knew it was there, why didn't you just say so? You always have to do it, don't you, make a big production out of everything?"

Stalking off, Lawrence continued his mental inventory of the house. "Even the TV is here," he commented. "Burglars always take the TV set."

"Who'd want it?" Emily asked. "It's just a fuzzy old black-and-white, and most of the time it only gets Channel 7."

"Maybe, but since when are thieves so choosy?"

Emily let her eyes wander around the room for a minute. Then, with a slightly trembly voice, she spoke again. "We've been robbed, Lawrence, but robbed of *nothing*. Nothing except my sand dollar necklace. Now that *is* creepy. Weird and creepy. Maybe the same people who murdered the man whose body I found broke in here."

With a shake of his head, Lawrence flopped down on the cushionless Danish sofa. Emily couldn't help smiling when she saw how uncomfortable he looked sitting on its wooden frame and exposed springs. "Conners was robbed of *everything,* this morning's paper said. TV, stereo, typewriter, tape recorder, two-way radio. Those kinds of thieves don't take the time to search through a house and then leave without taking anything."

Emily started tossing cushions back on the part of the couch where her brother wasn't sitting. "Stand up," she said, "and I'll put one under you. Maybe we scared them, caught them in the act. Maybe they were here about to start packing up what they wanted when they heard us coming. Or maybe . . . maybe they were looking for something special they hadn't found yet."

"Like a wall safe or valuable paintings? Not a chance," Lawrence answered. "And they couldn't have been here when we were coming up the hill or we'd've seen them leaving. This house has only one door, dummy. The front one."

"Well, they could have jumped from the window in Ma and Dad's room when they heard us."

Lawrence shook his head. "No, we'd have seen them running down the hill. No, there's something fishy about this whole thing. Even the door doesn't look like it's been forced open, and I'm sure you locked it when you left."

"But we never lock our door during the day," Emily protested, trying to remember if she'd pushed the button on the door handle as she ran out.

"You're telling me you left the door unlocked so anyone could walk right in and clean us out? No, Emily, that's just not the way it happened."

"What happened then? What happened?"

"Last night, you were all scared, triple-locking the door and whimpering about dead bodies and robberies. Then today you were scared because you thought you heard noises behind the house. You wouldn't have left here this morning without locking the door." Lawrence was frowning and staring at Emily with that mean-eyed look of his. She picked up an overturned chair, set it on its feet, and began backing away from him and from that look. "But I do have another idea . . ." he was saying as the phone began to ring.

Emily dashed past him and grabbed the receiver. "Hello!" she shouted.

"Emily?" said the voice on the other end. "Is that you? What are you yelling for? This is Dad. How's my girl? Did Lawrence get everything set up all right at the science fair?"

"Hi, Daddy," Emily said. "Is Ma there? Can I talk to her?"

"I haven't seen you in a week, I call from Oregon,

and all you can do is ask for your mom. I'm going to think you don't love me."

"I love you, Daddy, really I do, but I *need* to talk to Ma. Right now. It's important."

As Emily was pleading with her father, Lawrence had moved right next to her. He was standing there with one hand on the receiver, looking as if he was going to wrench it from her. His eyes were shooting a silent message in her direction. "Don't tell or I'll kill you!" his eyes were saying to her.

"What is it, Em?" her father asked. "What's wrong?"

Looking up at Lawrence, Emily started to loosen her grip on the phone. "I think my no-good brother wants to talk," she said. "He's pulling the phone away from me."

Lawrence started talking immediately. He turned his back on Emily and told his father all about plankton and about picking up his exhibitor's badge and his hopes for a first or second prize. But he didn't say a word about the house being torn apart. As he talked on and on, Emily stood there looking around at the mess and listening to Lawrence talk much faster and louder than usual.

Finally it was her turn to talk again. Lawrence's left hand was gripping her arm tightly as he let her take hold of the phone.

"Is everything all right, Em?" Joan Mendle asked. "Daddy said you have something important to tell me."

"I do," she said hesitantly.

"What?"

Emily squeezed her eyes shut. Then she couldn't see anything. But she could still feel—feel Lawrence's fingers bruising her arm. "Do . . . do you know what's white, has one horn, and gives milk? A dairy truck! Get it? *A dairy truck!*"

Emily really didn't want to get off the phone. She knew that trouble was coming. Lawrence had been about to tell her something before the call, and she knew she was going to have to listen to it when she hung up. She was right.

Without wasting any time on preliminaries, he started talking as soon as the receiver touched down. "I know how the house got all wrecked up, Emily, and I think you know, too!"

"How?" she asked, in a voice she knew was a little whiney. Lawrence absolutely hated that whiney tone, but she couldn't seem to help herself.

"You could have done it, Emily," he said, shaking one fist at her. "You—all by yourself—in all that time you had while I was picking up Dave and Ted and worrying that you weren't going to make it to the bus on time.

"Of course that's it. It took me a few minutes to put it all together. But that's it. Why you even set me up for it by telling me you heard someone outside and telling me to look out back!"

"But I didn't do it, Lawrence," Emily protested. "I didn't."

Lawrence squinted at her. "Who else would have been stupid enough to stage a robbery and not take a thing? You just did it to scare me and to get Ma and Dad to come home. Well, at least I kept you from lying to them on the phone. Emily, you've been asking for trouble ever since Ma left for Oregon, and it's gotten worse and worse. One thing after another. Especially since Dad's left. And now this—the whole house torn apart. You just think I don't notice things! Like today—today was a disaster—embarrassing me like that in front of my friends."

Emily twisted her hands together behind her back. "They thought I was cute. We laughed together."

"They weren't laughing *with* you, you idiot. They were laughing *at* you. They didn't really think you were cute. I didn't either. And now, you've pulled this stupid trick . . ."

"But I didn't! I keep telling you, I didn't. Listen, I bet it was Nettie. You know how she always says that it's the story of her life that nothing ever happens . . ."

"Don't give me that garbage," Lawrence interrupted. "It wasn't Nettie. It was you and it was a sick thing to do—to throw everything around and leave the door wide open all day. A real burglar could have just walked right in and cleaned out the whole place. Don't just stand there, looking guilty. Answer me! Just tell the truth and admit what you've done, will you?"

Emily kept twisting her hands and staring at her brother, noticing that his shoelace was untied again, that the second button from the top on his shirt was unbuttoned, that the tips of his ears were twitching.

"Answer me!" he yelled.

"But it wasn't me! It wasn't."

"Don't lie to me."

"I didn't do it. You must *believe* me, Lawrence," she begged, backing away from him again. Now she was against the kitchen counter and there wasn't any farther she could go, unless she was going to try and wedge herself into the vegetable bin. "My room was all torn up, too. There were real robbers here. Not me. Real criminals. I'm scared. I'm going to call Ma and Dad. Call them back and tell them about the house today and the body yesterday."

"No, you're not," Lawrence said, standing up and beginning to kick his way through the things strewn on the floor. "Only I have their number, and I'm not going to give it to you because *you* did this. You did it and it was dumb. So dumb only you could think up something like this. Where were you, Emily, when brains were passed out?"

Emily squatted down. She pulled the sneaker off her right foot and started to unlace the hiking boot she was wearing on her left one. Usually she loved to have Lawrence yell at her. But this was different. She felt all shaky inside. And very confused. "Maybe Carla did it," she mused. "As a joke. To give me some new material for my pencil-family stories. She could have done it, you know, because she knows where we hide the outside key."

"Carla Stiefel? Not a chance. She's got a good head on her shoulders. She wouldn't do a thing like that. Not even as a joke. *You did it.* I can tell by looking at you, and we aren't going to discuss it any more. Now, Emily, you'd better start cleaning up. Everything. I want everything in order before Nettie comes back from San Rafael. If she walks in and finds the house like this, she'll go to bed with a two-day migraine!"

Emily tugged at a stubborn knot in her boot lace. "When I was little, you were good to me. You walked me to school. You read to me, and you took me hiking on the mountain all the time. What's wrong now? Why do you hate me so much?"

"I don't hate you," Lawrence growled.

"Well, you act like it."

Lawrence put his hands on his hips. "What do you want me to do, Emily? Huh?"

"Talk to me. You never talk to me . . ."

Squinting, he looked down at her. "This is not the time to start discussing my feelings toward you."

"It never is," Emily said softly.

"You say I never talk to you, but I'm just not a big talker, and you know it. I never was. But you—you never shut up."

The knot came loose and Emily finished unlacing her boot. "All right then. I'll try not to talk so much. What else, Lawrence? Just tell me and I'll do it."

He scratched his head. "Well, you could stop stealing pencils to play with."

"I don't *play* with pencils," Emily protested, trying to keep her voice even. "I use them to help me with my stories."

"What stories?" Lawrence yelled. "You never write any stories! Never."

"In my head I do."

"That's not writing, Emily. Writing is putting things down on paper. You could do that, you know. Use up some of the extra energy and time you're wasting now on all your stupid pranks. It might do you good to try it. If you worked more, you'd talk less—and you might improve your mind a little. It could use it."

Emily leaned against the cabinet behind her. She could feel its stainless-steel handle pressing into her left shoulder. "Okay," she agreed tentatively, "you think I should talk less, stop playing with pencils, and start writing stories. Is that all?"

In silence, Lawrence looked down at her for a long moment. Then, speaking slowly, he answered her. "No, there's one more thing. *Grow up*."

"I'm not sure," Emily said with a frown. "I'm not sure I want to talk less or stop fussing with my pencils, or start writing stories down on paper. And I'm not at all sure I want to grow up. Especially if it means I'll turn all cranky like you. Even Carla's getting that way lately. She says her mom says it's the hormones changing . . ."

Lawrence ran his hands through his hair. "Spare me. Please spare me. If you think I'm going to stand around in this torn-up house and discuss Carla's mother's theories about hormones, you've got another think coming. Every time I ever try to talk about anything with you, I'm sorry afterward."

Lawrence was moving forward as he yelled at her. "You're impossible. Absolutely impossible. You tear apart the whole blasted house and then, instead of just admitting what you've done, you want to discuss why you think I hate you and you want to talk about my hormones!"

After Emily had lined up the tennis shoe and the boot next to one another on the floor, she was ready to answer. "Your idea of a good discussion," she said quietly, "is for me to agree with every single thing you say and do just what *you* want. That's not a discussion."

Now Lawrence was only inches from where Emily was crouching. He leaned down, grabbed her by the shoulders, and pulled her roughly to her feet. "Neither is this! This is not a discussion. This is an order. Clean up!" he yelled right into her face. "Everything! Now! Or I will shake you 'til your teeth rattle, pound your butt 'til you can't sit down. Clean up everything. Except for my room. I'm going in there by myself to be alone. Don't come near it. Don't knock on the door or open it or say one single word to me. Don't even offer me dinner. I won't want any. I'm going to stay in my room alone. Now clean up, stupid!"

Then, abruptly, Lawrence turned and stalked out of the room. He slammed his door. Emily stood there, wiping her face to get rid of the spit he'd sprayed at her in his anger, but she didn't move. For the longest time, she just stood there staring after him. Finally, she went to close and lock the front door, which was still standing wide open. Then, almost mechanically, she began doing as Lawrence had ordered. Puzzled and confused, she started picking up the incredible mess.

"Was it Carla?" she asked herself. "Carla and Jeff being funny in a weird way?" Emily stopped working long enough to dial the Stiefels' number, but there wasn't any answer so she went back to picking up. First, she took care of her own room. She stuffed her clothes back in the drawers and closet. She put the mattress back on the bed and remade it. Before she went on to the rest of the house, she did take a few moments to unpack the pencil families and Queenie from her knapsack and put them back under the mattress, in their usual hiding place.

Then she started on the main living area. She was feeling tired and thirsty, but, still, she was preoccupied. It might have been Carla, she decided, but if it wasn't, something really scary was going on. Who would break into a house, tear it apart, and leave without taking anything except her necklace? Emily was beginning to feel sorry for herself, too. Lawrence hadn't listened to her. All he had done was yell and order her to do all the picking up. It wasn't fair.

But she kept at it until everything began to have some semblance of order. The drawers and closets were messy on the inside, but at least things were up from the floor. The last job was the kitchen cabinets. She was a little more careful with them because she wanted to be able to find things when she was cooking. She had finished with the cans and cereal boxes and was rolling the potatoes back toward their bin, feeling very grumpy, when the phone started ringing.

She leaped up to answer it, sure it would be her parents calling back to ask why she'd sounded so odd before.

This time she'd tell them everything. Especially how awful Lawrence was being. It wasn't right to keep things from them, Emily decided as she lifted the receiver. Lawrence might be older—and smarter—but he wasn't always right.

Saying hello, she slid into the desk chair, waiting to hear her parents' warm, sympathetic voices. But she didn't hear them. All she heard was a deep, unfamiliar male voice asking, "Is this Western Union?"

"I'm sorry," Emily started to say. Then, for some perverse reason, she changed her mind. "Yes," she said in her most adult manner. "Wait, sir, if you please. I seem to have misplaced my pencil." She ran back to her room and grabbed Mrs. Ticonderoga from under her mattress. Then she rushed back to the desk. "Now," she said, "thank you so much for waiting. I am ready to take down your message."

"All right," said the man. "Here goes."

"Yes?" Emily said.

"My name is Arthur Sanger at 43 Willow Hill Drive in Mill Valley. My number is 383–3679. You got that?"

"Yes."

" 'Dear Walter,' " the man said. "You got that? Are you getting all this down?"

"Yes," Emily said. "Yes, I am. Your message starts 'Dear Walter.' Now, go ahead, sir . . ."

# 7

"Breakfast is ready," Emily called, putting a large platter of steaming pancakes on the table.

Emily wasn't at all sure why she'd bothered to make breakfast for Lawrence when he'd treated her so badly the day before. But it was morning, the sun was shining, and for some reason, Emily always felt good when she got up out of bed. Last night she'd been angry and upset. She and Nettie had spent most of the evening discussing all the possible reasons for a non-robbery robbery. They hadn't come up with any answers, however. Not even one. But this was the beginning of a new day and Emily was planning to climb up Mount Tam with Carla. That would make her feel wonderful. It would also help her to forget about dead bodies and robberies. In anticipation of the day's climb, she'd jumped out of bed not long after sunrise, dressed, straightened out her dresser drawers, packed her knapsack, and mixed up a large bowl of pancake batter.

She was sitting alone at the table when Lawrence stumbled into the room. He was wearing a pair of red-dotted pajamas with no buttons. They didn't have any buttons because Emily had snipped them off yesterday when she was picking up the mess and feeling angry at him for making her do it.

Lawrence looked out-of-sorts, Emily decided, but he always looked that way in the morning. It took him a long time to wake up. She stared at him, trying to decide just what he was going to do or say to her. To her disappointment, he didn't do anything or say anything. He just padded over to the desk where the phone and his microscope were. For a moment, Emily thought he was going to sit down and stare into his scope, ignoring the breakfast she'd prepared. But that wasn't what he had in mind. Instead, he lunged out and grabbed Mrs. Ticonderoga, whom Emily had carelessly left by the phone last night. Then tucking Mrs. Ticonderoga behind his right ear, he picked up the yellow tablet by the phone, and headed for his place at the table. As he was seating himself, he was squinting at the tablet, trying to decipher what was written there. " 'Dear Walter,' " he read aloud, in a puzzled voice. " 'All is forgiven. Your mother and I want you to come home. Let us know if you need money. Love, Dad.' "

Giggling nervously, Emily cut into the stack of green pancakes on her plate.

"What is this? What is this?" Lawrence yelled, trying to hold his pajamas together with one hand and waving the tablet wildly with the other.

Emily shrugged. "Western Union. This man called yesterday. He wanted me to take a message so I did." She braced herself, sure that her brother would yell even louder now, telling her what an awful thing she'd done. But he didn't. He just dropped the tablet with a pained expression on his face. Then he picked up his fork and speared a stack of pancakes.

He noticed the green color of the pancakes right away. Emily could tell by the way he poked them with the tip of his knife. She shouldn't have played another prank this morning. She knew that, but still, she had to punish Lawrence some more for accusing her of yesterday's robbery. Now as he examined the pancakes, Emily pressed her lips together tightly, trying not to laugh as she waited for him to explode.

But he didn't. After gazing at his plate for a long moment, he doused his portion of pancakes with syrup. Then he began cutting them up into methodical little squares and shoveling them into his mouth. When he finally said something, his voice was quite calm. "Green Mint Mouthwash?" he asked, talking with his mouth bulging with the nauseating green stuff. "Prell Shampoo? Candle wax? Arsenic?"

"Food color," Emily answered. "Just food color. Twenty-three drops of yellow and seventeen drops of blue. I wanted to do something outrageous—something that would make your breakfast a little more exciting."

Lawrence waved his arms through the air as he responded to her words. "More exciting? More exciting? You are driving me out of my skull."

Because he was waving his arms so wildly, Lawrence managed to turn his glass of milk over. It spilled into his plate, on top of the pancakes, but he didn't pay any attention to that. He kept right on talking. "I don't know what's going on in that crazy head of yours. Maybe finding a corpse has blown your mind. But if things don't improve we'll have to lock you up. That fake robbery yesterday—that was the worst. Unbelievable. Just wait 'til Dad and Ma come home. It was probably your fault that page 67 was missing from my science report. I work three months on it, and then hand it in with a page missing. Now I have to make a special trip into the city to deliver the page and then rush back to be at McHenrys by twelve, since I'm sitting for their boys today. Three of them, Emily, are easier to deal with than one of you. And they're all younger. Do you hear me?"

Emily still felt as if she were going to start laughing. When Lawrence yelled like this, he was so funny, she thought. His hair flapped all around, his nostrils flared, and he got bright red spots in the middle of each cheek. This morning he looked even funnier than ever because his buttonless pajama top kept coming open and threatening to slide off his shoulders.

Yes, she had done some aggravating things. She'd banged on the piano, put eggshells in his eggs, worn make-up and crazy clothes, dyed his pancakes green. But she hadn't been responsible for the missing page in his project or for the fake robbery. Lawrence was pretending to ignore her, but he couldn't really do it. He was, in his own way, paying attention to her—more attention than he'd ever done before. But she wasn't sure she was happy with what was going on. Now, she was beginning to see, she was going to be blamed for every single strange thing that happened in the Mendle house.

Emily was thinking all this as she pressed her lips together and watched Lawrence eating the green pancakes soaked through now by syrup and milk. It shouldn't have been funny, but it was. It would have been even funnier, she decided, if she'd given him a glass of her homemade root beer instead of just milk. She should have been worrying, but she felt like laughing. First she gave a little snicker. Then a tiny snorting sound escaped through her nose. Then a snortier snort, and before she knew it she was howling with laughter. Laughing so hard that tears were running down her face and dribbling in the corners of her mouth.

Lawrence wasn't laughing. His eyes were fixed on

her, almost shooting daggers like in the afternoon TV cartoons. What he did next seemed to Emily to be an episode right out of one of those cartoons. She watched it, took part in it, let it happen almost as if it were a cartoon—running in slow motion.

With one long-fingered hand Lawrence lifted a large brown earthenware pitcher from the center of the table. That was Nettie's pitcher, filled to the brim with water and ice. Nettie always drank a lot of ice water, especially when she was trying to ward off a migraine. Lawrence's fingers were curling around the handle of the pitcher. His thumb was braced against its side. With his lips clamped in a close thin line, he held the pitcher poised in the air. Emily saw it. She heard the ice cubes clinking against its side, and she knew exactly what was going to happen. Slowly, deliberately, Lawrence started pouring out the contents of the pitcher. And Emily felt it—every drop. Every last drop in the pitcher cascaded over her head, dripped through her ponytails and her clothes. The ice cubes came, too, bouncing off her head and shoulders.

When the pitcher was completely empty, Lawrence put it down calmly, picked up his fork, and began to finish off the green mush on his plate. Emily opened her mouth to scream, but no sound came out. She sat there with her mouth hanging open, feeling the icy water soak her hair, her shirt, her jeans, and listening to the ice cubes clatter against the floor as she wriggled with cold. She wanted to scream—to call desperately for Nettie—but then she didn't do it. She wasn't going to give Lawrence that satisfaction, she decided.

Instead, she jumped up and ran for the sink, leaving a trail of icy water dripping on the floor behind her. She grabbed for a sponge and a pan. Then she returned to the table, crawled down under it, and began mopping up the water. So much had soaked into her hair and clothes she couldn't understand how there had been enough left over to puddle on the floor. But it was there, and it seemed like an enormous quantity to be sponged away. Wipe—squish—wipe—squish. She kept sponging and wringing it out into the pan. At the same time, she kept lunging from side to side, trying to capture the slippery ice cubes.

Lawrence was still sitting at the table. She could see his pajama legs, his hairy ankles, his long, bony feet, and his empty, brown leather slippers. Emily smiled to herself as she noticed the empty slippers. Dropping the sponge into the pan, she decided she'd just have to do something about that empty pair of slippers. So, working quietly, she collected stray ice cubes and packed them into the toes of Lawrence's size-eleven slippers. She was careful not to put in too many—just enough. Then, smiling triumphantly, she backed out from under the table.

"I'm leaving, Nettie," Emily called, as she scrambled to her feet. She ran over to the sink to deposit the pan and sponge. "I'm meeting Carla by the firehouse. We're going hiking on Tam. See you at dinner."

At the sound of Emily's voice, Nettie came running flat-footed from the back of the house. "Gone all day? You sure you won't get lost up there?"

"Oh, no," Emily assured her. "I know just about every trail on the mountain. And I have my map, too. In the knapsack with my lunch. I'll be fine."

"Are you sure it's safe? Two children alone? What about rattlesnakes?"

Emily reached for her knapsack and started wriggling into its shoulder straps. "Oh, yes, big brown ones—lots of them with beady eyes and long, red forked tongues."

"Really?" Nettie asked, pushing her glasses back up on the bridge of her nose.

"No, no, no," laughed Emily. "I'm teasing. No, I've never seen any up there." She paused and reconsidered. "Well, *I've* never seen any, but Daddy and Lawrence thought they saw one once, but he was little and he slithered off. Not Lawrence—the snake."

Emily was giggling, but Nettie looked concerned. "Wait," she urged.

"Why?"

"Maybe you shouldn't go climbing that mountain alone. Maybe your Ma wouldn't like it."

"But when she's home I go all the time. She always lets me go," Emily protested.

"Well, when she's away, I'm in charge . . ." Nettie shook her head. "Listen—maybe I should call my niece in San Rafael—you know—Mary Lou, my sister's girl? She knows all about birds. Maybe she would go walking with you."

"Oh, no, no. Please don't call Mary Lou. She's nice, but please don't call her. It's all right. I'll be careful, and I'll have Carla to protect me. She's so smart and careful. She won't go *anywhere* that isn't safe. Don't worry, Netts. Don't. We'll be just fine. Okay? Okay? See you later?"

Nettie didn't look convinced, but she looked like she was tired of arguing, so Emily started toward the front door. Looking back over one shoulder, she noticed that Lawrence was still at the table. He was working on the crossword puzzle from the morning paper, completely tuned out to Nettie or to her. Mrs. Ticonderoga was still behind his left ear, but he was holding another pencil in his hand. A new one that Emily had never seen before. She squinted at it. A Dixon, she decided. She could, as a matter of fact, use a new Mr. Dixon. The present one had toothmarks all over his body. But she could do that later, after she came back from her hike.

Her hand was already on the doorknob when she realized that Nettie was sort of swaying back and forth near the couch. Swaying and tugging at her left ear.

"Hey, Netts, are you all right?" she called out.

Nettie kept tugging on her ear with one hand. With the other, she pushed up her glasses and began to massage her forehead. "Well . . . well, don't you worry now, hon. It's just my old head again."

Emily looked harder. Nettie was wearing one of her usual muu-muus, but her red hair, showing a lot of gray at the roots, was all stiff this morning. Uncombed, it stuck out around her head like a giant thistle. She looked as if she'd just climbed out of bed except that she had on her Foot Saver walking shoes. As Emily watched her, she shuffled over to the sink to pick up a paper bag. That was how Nettie stole other people's flowers, Emily knew, by carrying a paper bag along with her as she walked, a bag large enough to hold cut flowers and a pair of pinking shears. After a thorough examination, Emily decided that Nettie looked very peculiar. She would have liked to ask Lawrence to stop crosswording so he could see if Nettie were sick. But she didn't ask. She was determined not to talk to him anymore this morning.

"Maybe I shouldn't go," Emily said. "I'll stay here

with you, Netts, if you're not well. You certainly shouldn't try to go out walking."

"I thought maybe the fresh air would clear my head, but maybe I should stay here, try lying down. But you go on, hon, and have a good time. It was just the worrying about a robbery that wasn't a robbery and Lawrence saying it was you. But you wouldn't do a thing like that."

"Maybe Carla did," Emily offered. "As a joke. I'll ask her today. Now lie down and don't worry."

"Oh, I won't," Nettie said, trying to sound cheerful. "Besides, Lawrence will be here."

"No he won't. He handed in his project with one page left out. He's got to ride in on the bus and hand it in. Then he's going to McHenrys."

Nettie chuckled. "That's right, that's right. Brainy Lawrence forgot to count his pages. You know, Em, he's probably the dumbest smart boy I've ever met. Yes—he *is* the dumbest smart boy I ever met. Now run along, will you? I'll be fine or I'm not Nettie Hartperson from Amsterblessing Street."

"Nettie Hartperson from Amsterblessing Street?"

"Yes," Nettie replied waving one blue-veined hand in Emily's direction. "I was listening for news about the Conners case or other robberies on the radio, and I heard about a woman who changed her name from

Nancy Newman to Nancy *Newperson.* She said it was more liberated, and listen, hon, Nettie Hartperson likes to be liberated and keep up on all the new things. If your friend Carla could change her name, why not me?"

Emily stood in the doorway, undecided. Nettie was looking strange and talking strange. She wished Lawrence were paying attention. "Well . . . I'm going then . . ."

As Emily spoke, Nettie reached into her dress and extracted something that had been tucked into her brassiere. "Wait," she called.

"What?"

"I can't seem to open the pill bottle this morning. These blasted child-proof caps only make sense to a child. Could you, Em? Before you go. Maybe . . . maybe I'll take a double dose."

Emily opened the warm plastic pill bottle and handed it back. As she did this, she kept one eye on Lawrence who was getting up from the table. She edged back toward the door because she thought he was about to put on his slippers. But he didn't. Instead, he turned and padded off barefoot toward the bathroom. Nettie was getting a glass of water to take her pills. Or was it a glass of vodka? Emily couldn't tell the difference. Lawrence had left his crossword puzzle on the table. Emily ran over, thinking she might like to rip it to shreds, but as she reached for it, Fifteen Across caught her eye. "A magnificent bird of prey," it said. "An endangered species."

She took the Dixon pencil Lawrence had left on the table and printed five letters in the spaces for Fifteen Across. She pressed as hard as she could without breaking the point. "E-M-I-L-Y," she wrote in big dark letters. Then, reaching over one shoulder, she slid the pencil into the back of her knapsack.

"Bye," she said, stopping long enough to give Nettie a big hug. "Bye. Feel better."

Nettie frowned. "You're all wet," she mused.

Emily shrugged, having almost forgotten she was still wet from being doused with a full pitcher of ice water. "It's nothing," she insisted, skipping over to the door. "I was just a little sloppy when I brushed my teeth this morning."

Then she turned, ran out the door, down the steps and along the street toward the firehouse. She had better be long gone, she decided suddenly, before Lawrence came back from the bathroom. Back for his puzzle. Back for his pencil. Back for the slippers—the brown ones with the ice cubes melting inside them.

# 8

"Of course, Jeff and I didn't come in your house and throw things around. Really, Emily. That would be so childish. Besides, Jeff's been hostile all week. He's jealous, I think, that we found a dead body and he didn't, so he won't have anything to do with me."

Emily and Carla were heading up a steep, rocky trail. The trail followed a stream which was full of spring water gushing down the mountainside toward the lagoon. They had to talk very loud to hear one another above the splashing water.

"It's a mystery. A real mystery," Emily insisted, noticing a slender, pale green orchid-looking flower growing at the edge of the water. "Ever since the body, things have been strange."

"Well, you should have called the police about the robbery," Carla commented.

"Oh, I did. This morning. But they didn't sound too interested when they heard nothing had been taken."

"That's *all* they said?"

Emily frowned slightly. "Well, they did say they

might come by the house today, and I forgot to tell Nettie. Well, if they come—she'll be there."

Carla stopped walking and took several deep breaths. "Do we *have* to go uphill like this, Emily? Why didn't we take one of the easier trails? Look at you with that knapsack. It looks heavy, too heavy for going uphill. What's in there? Provisions for a month? This is so steep and I'm so out of breath."

Emily laughed. "That's because you're talking too much. Remember S.Y.B.? Save Your Breath."

"Well, it's hard," Carla said, "because you keep talking to me and being so overdramatic. Maybe Lawrence did it. Maybe he had some friends come in while you were in the city and mess it up just to scare you. With all the things you've been doing to him, I wouldn't blame him one bit."

Emily shook her head. "No, he doesn't have any friends except Ted and David and they were with us. Come on, Car-Car, let's keep walking or we'll never make it up to that cave. You go first, as slow as you want, and I'll follow you. Okay?"

Carla agreed and the girls started walking again. After a while, the trail crossed the stream and went up the other side of the canyon wall in a series of U-shaped switchbacks. In silence, the girls followed it. They had to be careful along this portion of the trail. The reddish rock under their feet was muddy in some spots and just slippery in others. Neither girl wanted to lose her balance and go rolling down the steep slope into the rocky stream bed.

Taking deep breaths, Emily looked all around as she walked. She noticed the dense forest of young fir trees around them, the lush ferns, and the delicate shade-loving wild flowers. She also watched the water cascading below her, watched it until something important occurred to her. Then, she tugged at Carla's sleeve. "The rangers say the salmon swim upstream here every February, but I've never even seen *one,*" she said. "I always miss important things like that. And like the tide changing. I'd like just once to see a salmon here."

Carla didn't answer. She was remembering to save her breath, Emily supposed.

There was little sunlight where they were and Emily was still chilly from Lawrence's dousing, but she didn't care. Being on the mountain always made her feel happy. Besides, she knew they would soon come out of the wooded canyon into an endless series of open, rolling grassy meadows that were flooded with sunlight. There, she'd dry out in fifteen minutes. She was thinking about the meadows when she heard the first noise.

"What was that?" she asked Carla.

"What?"

"That rustling, crackling noise behind us?" Emily stopped and looked back over her shoulder, but she didn't see anything.

"I didn't hear any noise," Carla said. "If there was a rustle, it was probably just a deer."

Trying to tighten the knapsack without taking it off, Emily tugged at one strap. "I wonder. I keep getting this creepy feeling, like I'm being followed. Like yesterday before I left for the city. And now there are creepy noises behind me. It all started with the corpse, you know."

"If you want to know what I think," Carla said, without turning anything but her chin back toward Emily, "I think you're imagining things. You spend just too much of your time listening to things, looking at tiny unimportant little details and adding them all up the wrong way. My mom says that the trouble with you, Em, is . . ."

"Shut up."

". . . the trouble with you, Em, is that you're too far into unimportant little junk like your pencil families and too far away from big stuff like setting goals for yourself and . . ."

Emily kicked at a rock and sent it speeding downhill to the stream where it landed with a satisfying splash-thunk. "The trouble with you, Carla, is that you've come out hiking with sneakers instead of boots and with holes in the heels of both your socks and you're going to get blisters today."

Carla giggled. "See? That's just what I mean. Just what I was saying."

"Oh, shut up," Emily said again.

"Do we have to keep climbing?" Carla asked, happy that Emily had given her another chance to complain about the steep trail.

"Yes."

Begrudgingly, Carla agreed and in silence the two girls went on. Emily refused to talk because she wanted to be able to listen for suspicious noises. She had heard something. She was sure of it. There continued to be a lot of strange cracklings, but as many times as she twisted her head to look back, she never caught a glimpse of anything. Of anything but fir trees, ferns, and a twisting reddish trail which dropped steeply behind her.

"Maybe it's just my imagination," she told herself, after a while. "A forest is always full of rustle-y noises." She almost managed to convince herself that the danger was imaginary. Almost but not quite. That's why she was so anxious to get out of the woods and into the open meadows. There, no one could follow her unobserved. At last, they reached the edge of the meadows. Emily took one final look into the rustling dimness behind her, but she still didn't see anything.

The girls kept on walking until they were well away from the shadows of the forest. Then they climbed up onto a grassy knoll and threw themselves down in the prickly-soft, long green grass. Rolling meadows were all around them. Below, at the edge of the forest, Emily saw wild lilac bushes fuzzy with bees. And below the forest, a mile downhill, she could see the sandspit of Stinson Beach, the Bolinas mesa, Duxbury Reef and the ocean with its white line of breakers. They weren't quite high enough to see the lagoon.

After a few minutes, Emily could feel herself beginning to relax. "Beautiful, beautiful," she crooned. "This mountain has *everything*. Canyons, streams, meadows, caves, forests, views . . ."

"And mysterious rustling strangers following ten-year-old girls," Carla said.

Emily laughed. "Well, I don't see anybody now. I *was* imagining things. We're alone, Carla, all alone here in the meadows."

And they were. Almost. Emily had hardly gotten those words out of her mouth when the Boy Scouts appeared over the rounded bump of a hill behind them.

There were six of them, dressed in short khaki pants with scarves around their necks and packs—huge packs—on their backs. To Emily, they looked a little fat and pale, like city kids out for their first walk in ten months.

They were sweating and panting as they approached.

"Hey, girls," one of the boys yelled.

"Hey, boys," Emily called back. Then she and Carla looked at one another and laughed.

The Scouts kept on coming closer until they were right behind Emily and Carla. "Either of you know how to find the Dipsea Trail from here?" a short, orange-haired boy asked.

"She knows," Carla said, pointing at Emily.

"The Dipsea!" Emily laughed. "The Dipsea! Did you wander all the way up here thinking you were on the Dipsea?"

Six tired-looking, perspiring Scouts nodded their heads up and down. "Yeah, we got separated from our leader and we can't seem to find the way down. We got these thirty-five-pound backpacks, you see, because we're conditioning for a Sierra climb next month. Can you help?"

Emily pulled out her ragged-edged, orange-covered mountain map and showed the six boys where they were and what they'd done wrong. She explained it to them over and over. They listened, nodding their heads up and down and wiping at their faces with the pointed ends of their scarves.

At last, they seemed to understand. "Down through the woods—right there—about half a mile. Then cross the stream and take the trail to the right but not the deer trail. Right? And it will take us all the way to Stinson. Okay?"

With a few more okays and some good-byes, the boys walked off. "So much for mysterious strangers," Carla laughed, turning from her stomach to her back.

Emily nodded. "I guess you're right," she said. "Let's eat here, and then we'll climb on up to the cave. You'll like it, Car-Car, really you will. A cave with its own spring. It would be a great place to run away to. No one would ever find me. Except Lawrence maybe. He knows about the cave, too."

Emily dumped out the contents of her knapsack—a sandwich, a hard-boiled egg, a can of apple juice, and a big jumble of yellow pencils.

Carla groaned. "Pencils! Pencils! I can't stand it. Even up here."

Emily unwrapped her tuna sandwich and bit into it absentmindedly. Using her free hand, she started to regroup the pencils, separating them into their proper families. "I promised them an Easter-week picnic. And all the money raised goes to help support the orphans," she said. "Anyway, I think better on my stories when I have the pencils to look at. Mrs. Ticonderoga was dragged off to jail again, and I haven't been able to bail her out, but I've got this new Dixon I took from Lawrence this morning."

"Is that so?"

"Yes, and Carla, I just found out he's the long-lost brother of the present Mr. Isadore Dixon. Konrad—with a *K*. I hope it won't cause any family troubles when he moves in with the rest of the Dixons."

Carla had pulled off her sneakers and socks and was busy picking at a blister on her right heel. It was obvious that she wasn't really listening to Emily's pencil-family saga, but Emily didn't care. Her sandwich tasted good, and looking at the pencils kept her from thinking about things like being followed and about why someone would want to ransack their house and not take anything.

After a while, Carla looked up, frowning over at the pencils with great superiority. Then, suddenly, she rolled over and grabbed one. "Where did you get this?" she asked.

Carla was holding the Queen high up over her head. In the bright sunlight, its shiny surface shone like a glinting beacon, sending signals out all through the meadows.

Emily stuffed the whole hard-boiled egg into her mouth at one time. She looked out over the meadow dotted with golden poppies and smoky blue lupine. She kept trying to hold her lips together, but yellow crumbs of yolk dropped on her jeans as she squished the egg between her teeth.

"Where did you get this gold pencil?" Carla repeated.

"Found it," Emily mumbled, choking down the last of the egg and brushing away the crumbly yolk.

" 'Blythe Queen,' " Carla said thoughtfully. "What does that mean?"

"Just a brand name—like Eberhard-Faber or Parker," Emily answered. Then she decided to change the subject. She didn't really want to tell Carla that she had taken the pencil at the lagoon, taken it from the bag by the body. "Come on, Car-Car. Eat. You haven't even started, and we can't just lie here all day. Not if you want to see the cave."

"How *do* you know where you're going up here?" Carla said, opening her sandwich bag at last. "I will never figure out how you know. When I look down at the ocean, I know that we live down there. But we could fall over a cliff or end up wandering around for weeks without getting down. How *do* you know?"

"I just do, that's all. I notice *details*. Remember? I see old stumps, bends in the trail, a piece of broken-down fence. I just look hard and remember things, that's all."

"It's a waste, you know," Carla declared.

Emily snuggled down into the long grass and rolled some of her pencils back and forth, idly. "Well, remembering is the best thing I do," she said. "Some people like you and Lawrence are just smart. Really smart—book smart, school smart. But I'm just kind of dumb." She smiled at Carla. "Lovable, but dumb."

"My mom says if you'd only take some of the *energy* you put into . . ."

Emily was only half-listening. She had learned to tune out rather quickly when Carla started offering psychiatric opinions which might or might not have come from her mother. As Carla droned on, Emily was staring down toward the edge of the woods. She thought she saw some hikers there. Two or three of them—back in the shadows of the trees. "Look, people," she said, interrupting Carla. "Down there."

"So?" Carla answered, obviously annoyed at being cut off in mid-sentence. "We already saw the Scouts. Maybe they're coming back. Or maybe it's some other hikers. This is Easter week, you know. You think we're the only people on the mountain and it's just yours?"

Emily started packing up her pencils, tossing them with a wooden clatter into the bottom of her knapsack, but she never took her eyes off the shaded figures down in the forest. "Why do they keep lurking there?" she asked. "What do they look like to you?"

Carla squinted, shading her eyes from the sun with one hand. "College kids? Hippies? How should I know?"

Carla had eaten only half of her sandwich. Now she was taking big slurping bites out of an apple and wiggling her toes at the same time. Emily kept her eyes fastened on the people in the woods. She couldn't figure out why anyone would keep lingering there in the shade with the sunny meadows just in front of them. One of the hikers was wearing something that disturbed her. Something whitish—like a vest, maybe.

Finally, Emily couldn't stand it any longer. "Put on your shoes," she ordered Carla. "I'm not kidding. I think we're about to be kidnapped by those people."

Carla just laughed and took another slurpy bite out of her apple. "Another pencil-family story comes to life," she teased.

Emily grabbed her by the arm and pulled her to her feet. "I'm *not* joking," she whispered fiercely. "See that white—like a vest? There was a girl at the lagoon, standing looking at the body, who looked like that. I saw her because she was staring at me."

"So? Lots of girls have rabbit vests. Macy's had a special on them last month. I saw the ad in the paper. Why should anyone who'd been at the lagoon, seeing the body, care about *you?* My mom would say you're getting paranoid."

Emily didn't know what paranoid meant, but she did know that she was getting a panicky feeling in her chest. She kept wanting to swallow and she couldn't quite do it. She was going to start drooling in another minute, she decided. Those people *were* interested in her. They *were* coming after her. She wasn't imagining things. She wanted to shout for help. But at the same time, she knew it wouldn't do any good because there wasn't anyone to help.

But, still, the word was pounding through her head. "Help! Help! Help!" She looked around. She wasn't calling. She was still trying to swallow her mouthful of saliva. Carla wasn't shouting either, but she was pointing up the hill behind them.

Emily looked where Carla was pointing. It was the Boy Scouts again, all six of them, coming back over the crest of a hill and yelling, "Help! Help! Help!" Somehow, despite Emily's careful directions, they'd loused up again and come around in almost a complete circle.

Emily took one more look down at the figures lurking at the edge of the woods. Then she jumped up and down and began to wave her hands wildly. "Over here," she shouted. "Come over here," she yelled, motioning to the fat boys in short pants. "I'll show you the way to the beach. I'll even walk with you—all the way down."

Carla's face brightened. "You mean we won't have to climb up to that cave?"

"That's right," Emily said softly. "We'd better do a good turn for the Boy Scouts. They'll never find their way down without me. They might fall over a cliff or get bitten by a snake."

The Scouts were almost next to them now. Emily looked back at the edge of the woods, but she couldn't tell if anyone was still lingering there. Funny dark circles swelled in the air before her as she tried to look from the bright sunlight into the dim woods.

"You really know the way down, kid?" one of the Scouts asked her. "You're not putting me on, man?"

Emily laughed and lunged for her knapsack. "Every trail on the mountain," she bragged. "I'm not putting you on, man."

Then, together, they all started back down toward the beach—Emily, Carla, and six tired, perspiring, lost Boy Scouts with thirty-five-pound packs on their backs. Emily was humming to herself as she walked. No one would kidnap her today.

# 9

"Lawrence, Lawrence," Emily shouted, pushing open the unlocked door at McHenrys and barging right in. "I was being followed on the mountain. Carla and me. By two—or maybe three—suspicious people. I think they were going to kidnap us!"

Lawrence was sitting in the middle of the living room floor, engrossed in a chess game he was playing with nine-year-old Willy McHenry. "Huh?" he answered, looking up at the sound of her voice.

"I'm going to take your knight," threatened Willy.

Lawrence looked at the chessboard again. "If you do, I'll take your queen," he told the boy.

"Lawrence!" Emily called again. "Did you hear what I said about being followed?"

"Why don't you move this pawn up two spaces instead?" Lawrence suggested to Willy. Then he nodded up at Emily. "Sure, I heard you. But right now—this week in particular—you're suffering from a serious credibility gap."

Emily wasn't at all certain what Lawrence had just

said, but she wasn't about to stop pleading with him. "You've got to believe me. They *were* following me. I'm scared, and I thought you'd want to know right away. I'm so scared, Lawrence. You must *do* something."

Lawrence recrossed his legs and frowned down at the chessboard.

"Please, Lawrence, please . . ."

"Emily," he sighed. "I can't concentrate with you bellowing at me. I've got enough to do with three little boys on my hands. You are not being followed. Now, why don't you run on home and let Nettie look after you, huh? No, Willy—move the rook instead. That's right." Lawrence shook his head so that his fine, straight hair slid back from his eyes. With a pained expression, he looked up at Emily. "Just like the strange crackling noises around the house yesterday morning. I believed you then. I even checked it out for you. Remember? But it was a phony—all part of the set-up for the phony robbery. And you also had a fake broken ankle. So injured yesterday you could hardly walk and well enough this morning to go out hiking. No one has been following you, Emily. And no one in his right mind would want to kidnap you. This is not a pencil-family world. Now—go home."

Emily dropped her knapsack to the floor and let herself sink down into the nearest soft chair. She kept right on talking, half to herself now. "Finding the body started all this. The body and the pencil. A Queen and a body."

Willy McHenry was listening to her. His eyes opened wide. Emily looked down at his small, thin, tanned body, at the way he cocked his head to one side when he spoke. He still had a jack-o'-lantern grin, she noticed, because half of his teeth were still growing in. "I wish I'd found a body," he said. "Tell me about it."

"Pay attention, Willy," Lawrence said. "Go home to Nettie, Emily. I've got three boys here to look after and that's about all I can handle."

"What three boys?" Emily asked. "I only see Willy."

But no one answered her. The two boys on the floor—one big and intense, one little and intense—just sat there with shoulders hunched, staring down at the chessboard. Emily sat watching them for a minute or two. Then a noise at the back of the house attracted her attention, and she went to look for the two younger McHenrys. She found them both in the hall bathroom.

Five-year-old Rob was lighting matches one after another and dropping each one into a sinkful of water, listening to the hissing sound they made. "See my rockets," he told Emily, looking up at her through his smudgy little tortoise-rimmed glasses. As he talked to her, he lighted another match and dropped it in the basin. "You look funny," he told Emily. "Sleepy-funny. And why are your fingernails so long?"

Emily rumpled his dark blond hair with one hand as she looked down at the enormous pile of burnt-out matches floating in the sink. Of the three McHenry boys, Rob was Emily's favorite. He noticed things—like she did.

Rob's matches were not the source of the noise she'd heard from the living room. It was two-year-old Jamey causing the noise. He was in the bathroom behind Rob, and he was very busy, too. In a methodical two-year-old way, he was dropping plastic soldiers into the toilet and flushing them away. One at a time, over and over again, he flushed away soldiers, telling each one of them, "Bye-bye. Bye-bye."

Emily didn't bother to call for Lawrence. Some baby-sitter he was. He was so unobservant, Emily decided, he could probably walk right into the bathroom to use the toilet without noticing anything unusual. He'd just thank Jamey for flushing it and Rob for having a basin of water ready for him to wash his hands.

At least for the time being, Emily thought she'd better take charge of the younger ones. With patience, she persuaded Rob to give Jamey all the rest of the unused books of matches. Then, together, the three of them watched as Jamey flushed the matchbooks down the toilet.

"Bye-bye," Jamey said. "All gone."

The toilet gurgled in a suspicious choked-up manner, and its surging water rose right up to the lip of the bowl as Emily and the two little boys watched. Emily didn't really even care if it overflowed. "If it does," she told herself, "Lawrence will have to clean it up. I'm not the baby-sitter around here." When it didn't spill over after all, she was almost disappointed.

Taking each of the younger McHenrys by a hand, Emily led them out of the bathroom and back to their bedroom. "How about a story?" she suggested. "I could tell you what happened to the pencil families this week." To illustrate her tales, she brought her knapsack full of pencils to their room, too. Then with the two boys sitting in her lap, she told them about baby Lucinda being kidnapped and rescued and about the pencil picnic on Mount Tam. She didn't feel scared or shaky any more as she sat there with two warm little bodies in her lap. Maybe she'd just stay at McHenrys the rest of the afternoon, she decided.

After a while, Jamey went to get his blanket. He began rubbing one corner of it in his ear.

"He's sleepy," Rob told Emily. "He needs his nap, but he can't have it yet."

"Why not?" Emily asked.

"Because," Rob answered, pushing his glasses on top of his head, "we haven't had lunch yet."

"No lunch," exclaimed Emily. "That Lawrence! He's a real creep. Come on, guys. I'll fix you lunch. Would you like that?"

"Yes," Jamey said. "Cookies."

Emily laughed and hugged him. "Cookies—and other things, too. You know, Rob, Lawrence is a lousy sitter. Your Ma shouldn't leave you all here with him so much. What does she do anyway? Is she going to school, finding herself like Carla says my Ma is doing?"

Rob shook his head. "No, she goes shopping. And she's not finding her, Em. She's trying to lose us."

Grinning, Emily tossed her pencils back into the knapsack. Rob McHenry said such incredible things, she told herself, someone should write a story about him. As she was thinking about this, Rob said something else. Something very ordinary for a five-year-old.

"Stick 'em up," he called reaching into his pocket and drawing out a shiny black gun with a red, rubber-tipped dart sticking out of the barrel. "Stick 'em up," he repeated.

"Oh, you're scaring me," Emily squealed, raising her hands to play along with his game. About that time, something hit her hard on the back. Another red-tipped dart. This one had been fired from an identical pistol which was being held by baby Jamey. "Bang-bang," he said.

"Hey, cut it out," Emily complained to Jamey. "Those

things hurt. Rob, Jamey shouldn't have a toy like that. He might get someone in the eye or something."

"It's not his," Rob said. "It's Willy's. The 7-Eleven had them on sale this week."

Emily sighed, took the shiny dart pistols away from both boys, and led them toward the kitchen. As they walked by the living room, Emily could see that the chessboard had been abandoned. Now Lawrence and Willy had their heads bent together over a crossword puzzle. Willy kept grinning up at Lawrence. "What's a seven-letter word meaning admiration that starts with 'r' and ends with 'ct'?" Lawrence asked.

"Respect!" Willy called out, licking his lips with pleasure.

"Right you are."

"Now a ten-letter word meaning an inconsiderate and cruel person."

"L-A-W-R-E-N-C-E," Emily volunteered.

Willy shook his head at Emily and flashed her his jack-o'-lantern grin. "That's dumb," he said. "Lawrence only has eight letters."

Emily put her hands on her hips and tried to look as tall as possible. First she gave Willy a scathing look and then she turned on her brother. "Lawrence, these kids haven't had lunch and it must be three o'clock already. I'm going to fix it for them."

"Oh, go home," Lawrence muttered. "I was just about

to make them something anyway. How about some Campbell's tomato soup, boys? That's my culinary specialty, you know, and I'll fix it because you've all been so good this morning. Come on, fellows. Go home, Emily."

Emily didn't take very long to make up her mind. She wasn't going to start letting Lawrence try to humiliate her in front of Willy McHenry. She'd just get her knapsack, walk out the door, and leave Lawrence to do the cooking. Lawrence—cook? Ridiculous. She chuckled to herself as she thought about it.

She didn't say good-bye to Lawrence or to Willy. That Willy—he was just a bratty little nine-year-old who thought he was a lot smarter than she was. He *was* a lot smarter than she was, Emily realized, but he still annoyed her.

"Bye, Rob," she called on her way out. "Hey, do you know why the elephant wore blue tennis shoes?"

"Because his red ones were in the laundry," answered Rob. "That's an old one."

Rob was using the electric can opener to open the soup can for Lawrence as he answered her. "Be careful not to cut yourself on the lid," she cautioned him. "Bye again. Bye-bye, Jamey."

Then Emily shouldered her knapsack and walked out the kitchen door. But she wasn't even halfway down the back steps when the yelling began. Her brother was yelling at Rob. "You threw out the can, stupid. How can I make soup without the can? Run outside to the bottom of the garbage chute and get the can. I need it. The directions are on it."

When Emily reached home, she was still chuckling to herself, thinking of Lawrence trying to take care of those boys, knowing he'd let the tomato soup boil and curdle the milk. "Tomato soup is his specialty," she giggled. "Ha!"

The phone was ringing as she walked up the front steps. It was ringing and ringing. She ran in the door, over to the table, and grabbed it. "Hello? Hello?" she said. But it was too late. Disappointed, she let the receiver fall back into the cradle.

"Nettie, Netts?" she called. But there wasn't any answer. The house was strangely quiet. Slowly, she went from room to room, looking everywhere—even in the closets, under the bed, and behind the shower curtain. But Nettie wasn't there. Not Nettie or anyone else. Emily was on her hands and knees peering under her parents' bed when the phone rang again. She slid out, reached up, and grabbed it. "Hello?"

The voice on the other end was very faint. "I have to leave a message. Who is this?"

Emily stood up. "This is *not* Western Union," she declared. "To send a telegram, you have to dial 800 first."

Just as Emily was about to slam down the phone, the voice at the other end got a little stronger. "Em, is that you, hon?"

"Nettie? Is that you? Where are you? What's wrong?"

"Well . . ." Nettie answered. "I seem to be at the police station."

Emily sank down on the bed so hard that it bounced and squeaked. "I can't hear you," she shouted into the phone. "Talk louder. Did you say you were at the police station?"

"That's right."

"What do they have you there for? For stealing flowers?"

There was no immediate answer from the other end.

"Nettie," Emily yelled, "are you still on the line?"

"Yes . . . well . . . no, it wasn't for the flowers," she mumbled. "I can't seem to hear you too well. I left my glasses back on Officer Alanson's desk, and I just don't hear as well without my glasses. I think maybe . . . maybe I'm here because I took one pill too many. I felt very shaky at the house, you see. When I was talking to this handsome policeman—the one you called about the robbery who came to the door to check."

Emily sat on the bed, staring out the window, seeing the familiar late afternoon fog seep in over the lagoon. "You still haven't told me how you got to the police station."

"Well, it's a long story . . ."

"Nettie, what kind of trouble *are* you in?" Emily asked, jumping to her feet. "Listen, I'll get Lawrence. He's smart and he'll know what to do. Tell me your number and exactly where you are and I'll have him take care of everything. Now don't worry, Netts. He's not dumb like me. He'll do everything . . ."

"It's not like that, Em. And besides that, you're not dumb! You're the smartest dumb person I ever met. There's more than one kind of smart. More than one kind."

"What does that mean?" Emily demanded. "More than one kind of smart? Lawrence's smart is what you need. Now tell me *exactly* where you are."

"In a phone booth—454-7676—at the police station in San Rafael, but I'm not in trouble, hon. I'm just sleepy—like I took one pill too many, but I told you that already, didn't I?"

"But, Netts, your voice sounds funny. It keeps fading in and out."

"Oh, well, that's just because I keep poking my head out of the booth to see the officer and see if my sister's here yet. The officer—Officer Alanson—he understands because his mother gets migraines and he's been so kind."

Emily was aware that the hand holding the phone was all sticky with perspiration. "What are you *doing* at the police station? Come home. I don't want to stay here alone."

"Drinking lukewarm coffee and waiting for my sister to come from Greenbrae to pick me up. Lukewarm coffee is what Mrs. Alanson takes. Not ice water—and never liquor. And the officer says maybe his mother might like one of my Hawaiian dresses and how much do I charge. You see, I asked him to drive me here to the station because it's closer to my sister's."

Emily could feel tears welling up in her eyes. "But you *must* come home. I don't want to stay here alone, Nettie."

"Well, it won't be for too long. You can stay with Lawrence at McHenrys. I'll take a taxi home from my sister's later or early tomorrow morning. Or maybe Officer Alanson will drive me back. This is all very exciting, Em. I feel like I'm part of one of your pencil-family stories. Me with a handsome young policeman taking care of me and calling me 'Miss Hartperson.' I might even change my hair color. Get a new dye job. Would that be a good idea? And maybe you could even write a story about us."

"Nettie! Nettie! Don't act crazy. Come home. You're

supposed to be here taking care of me! Nettie!" Emily pleaded.

"Oh, I will, tonight—or tomorrow, hon. Now be a good girl, will you, and stay with Lawrence."

"But what about the robbery, Nettie? And now I think I'm being followed, too. Maybe the robbers will come back. Put the policeman on the phone—that Officer Alanson—and let me talk to him. I'll tell him all that's going on. He should hear it from me."

After a long silence Nettie answered. "All your yelling is making my head hurt again. My poor head. But you don't need to talk to Dennis—I mean Officer Alanson—because I did. And he says the fake robbery was just a kid's prank. It won't happen again—and it's not dangerous. Now don't worry your pretty little head any more."

"Please, Nettie!"

"I'm having trouble hearing you, hon, without my glasses. I mean, I hear the shouting, but the words aren't all that clear, and I'm afraid my three minutes are up and I hate to ask Dennis for another dime. So I'll see you later, hon. Be good."

Then the phone clicked and Emily was left standing there holding a dead line. For a moment, she just stood there helplessly. Then she slammed down the receiver, picked it up and dialed McHenrys. Willy answered. "Let me talk to Lawrence," she barked.

After a long pause, Willy came back to the phone. "Lawrence can't come," he told Emily. "He's got Jamey on the potty."

"*You* go watch Jamey on the potty," Emily ordered, "and tell Lawrence this is important. Really important. Nettie's at the police station."

After what seemed like an interminable wait, Lawrence picked up the phone. "Yeah?"

"Nettie's at the police station in San Rafael."

"Damn it, Emily," Lawrence yelled. "I've had enough of your lies and pranks. Nettie's not at the police station—so don't start telling me she's been put in jail for stealing flowers or something. She's out walking. She'll be home in a little while, so don't bore me with your dumb pencil-family story stuff."

Then, abruptly, he slammed down the phone.

Emily dialed again. Again, Willy answered. "Give me Lawrence," she demanded.

"He won't talk," Willy said. "As soon as he's through with Jamey, he's going to look through my baseball cards with me. He says you're a dumb brat and that you should get lost."

"Did he really say that?" Emily demanded. "Did he?"

"Yes, Emily. He said you should get lost." With these words Willy finished the conversation. Then he hung up without waiting for her to say any more.

Emily was furious. Absolutely enraged. Nettie was

gone. She was being followed by mysterious strangers. The house had been broken into, and Lawrence wouldn't listen.

"I'm *not* going to stay here by myself," she muttered. "Not for five minutes more. Lawrence said to *get lost*—and that's exactly what I'm going to do."

# 10

"Carla, is that you?" Emily asked, twisting the phone cord between her fingers. "I have something very important to tell you—but you *must* promise me you can keep a secret."

"Tell me what it is first," Carla insisted.

"No, you must promise—like I promised for you after you read your mom's old love letters."

"All right. I promise. What is it?"

Emily's voice was whispery. "I'm running away from home."

"Oh, is that all?" Carla asked. "Just *that* again. What time should we expect you? Are you bringing your sleeping bag or should I pull out the trundle?"

Emily stared out the front window. Through the layers of misty afternoon fog, she could just make out the dim shape of a large freighter heading north up the coast. "No, this is different," she said at last. "I'm going up the mountain for a few days alone. Just me. Nettie's at the police station in San Rafael, on the way to her sister's, and Lawrence's at McHenrys, and he won't even talk to me, and I can't find the number for my folks' motel in Lawrence's piggy room. So I'm leaving. I can't stand it here any longer—strange people, being followed—everything."

"Slow down. Stop a minute," Carla urged. "You're not really going back up on Tam. You went crazy up there today when you thought those hikers might be following us."

"This will be different," Emily said. "It's getting dark already. The fog is coming in, and no one but me knows the way to the cave. I'm going to climb up a secret way, in dark clothes. I'll be safe up there. Safer than here alone in this house. But you mustn't tell Lawrence where I am. I'm going to make him sorry for the way he's been treating me. But when you talk to him, you might make sure he does something about getting Netts home from her sister's."

"Come on, Emily, you're not really going up there at night alone."

"No, I won't be alone."

"Now who would be dumb enough to go with you?"

"The pencil families. And we'll be fine—all of us."

"Emily? Emily?" Carla shouted into the phone. "I think you're having a nervous breakdown. You'd better come over here right now. Mom will be home from work in half an hour."

"No, I'm going off alone . . ."

"Well, at least stop by here, will you? We could look

after you for the night. You'd be safe from everything here, you know. Perfectly safe."

Emily didn't answer immediately. She knew she wasn't going to accept Carla's offer. But, for a moment, it *was* tempting.

"Emily?"

"I'm here."

"Well, are you coming? You want me to run over and help you carry your stuff? And Mom will help. She'll be wonderful. She'll help you analyze your problems to find out why you keep thinking you're being followed."

"No!" Emily shouted into the phone. All she needed was a few hours with Carla's mother. Right now, she'd do anything to avoid talking with one more person who wouldn't believe her or take her seriously. "I hate you, Carla, and I hate your mother, too. I know exactly what I'm doing. I'll be safe on Tam, and I'll be punishing Lawrence at the same time."

"Stay right where you are, Em. Don't move. Or maybe you should lie down with a cold cloth on your head. You might put your feet up higher than your head, too. Stay there—I'm coming right over."

"Don't bother," Emily said with a bitter chuckle. "I'll be long gone."

Then, without waiting for Carla's reply, Emily slammed down the phone, picked up her already-packed knapsack, Lawrence's goosedown sleeping bag, and walked out the door.

Right from the beginning, she was careful to make sure she wasn't being followed. Instead of starting up one of the trails, she crawled into a thicket of dense brush near the white church and started climbing there. It wasn't easy. Every step she was getting prickled by thistles and blackberry vines. Making progress was difficult—especially with a knapsack and sleeping bag. There was a lot of poison oak there, too, but that didn't worry her since she never seemed to get it. "Anyone who tries to follow me up this way," she told herself with a self-satisfied shake of her head, "will probably die of poison-oak itching."

She was pleased that the fog was probing into the mountain canyons because it was shutting out the light, making it very dark for four o'clock. Down at the beach, it would have been cold in the fog, but in the protected gullies of the mountain, it was quite comfortable. Emily was warm anyway—warm from climbing and from the excitement of running off alone to a secret cave.

From time to time, she would stop, stand very still, and listen. But she didn't hear any suspicious sounds that didn't belong to the woods. Only a few bird calls and froggy crickety sounds. But no footsteps. She was safe. This was very different from climbing up a three-foot-wide trail in the middle of the day making a racket as she argued with Carla. No one—absolutely no one—would be able to track her now. And, still, she wasn't that far from the Matt Davis Trail. It was below her on her left, and below it was the rushing stream. Faintly, if she strained, she could hear its watery whir.

After a while she came out of the thicket and began climbing up a rocky hillside covered with dense young fir trees. She couldn't seem to climb that way with the knapsack and sleeping bag on her back, so she kept shoving them a little way ahead of her, hoping they wouldn't roll back. Then she'd inch her way hand over hand to reach them. Occasionally, she was able to grab hold of a rocky ledge to pull herself, but a lot of the rock was too crumbly to grab. So, most of the time, she found herself gripping the rough, skinny tree trunks like they were Junglegym bars and using them to pull herself higher up the hill. To keep from slipping, she had to brace her feet against the trunks and against protruding tree roots.

It didn't take long for her hands to become reddened and raw or for the muscles in her armpits to start aching. Two of her long fingernails had broken off and her shoulders hurt from lifting and throwing her gear. But, strangely enough, she still felt good. She was going up *her* mountain to *her* cave, leaving Lawrence to worry about Nettie, about who had tried to rob their house, about where she had gone. Now, for the first time since she'd found the body at the lagoon, she wasn't going to worry about anything.

"I've always wanted to spend the night here," she told herself, heaving the knapsack and sleeping bag one more time. "And now I will."

She was very excited about the whole thing. It was going to be a wonderful, crazy adventure. Lawrence would not be able to ignore this. He'd worry, be frantic about her, have an awful time searching for her—and she'd be having so much fun. There was nothing on Mount Tam to scare her. Not tonight. Not even the darkness. She wasn't the least bit afraid of the dark. She never had been.

But despite her enthusiasm, climbing up a mountain without a trail was exhausting. She had to keep stopping to catch her breath. One time when she was leaning back against a tree trunk, she looked down by her feet and saw a banana slug—a disgusting six-inch yellow-green banana slug crawling up the hillside. She hated banana slugs. Ordinarily, she would have grabbed a stick and used it to fling the slug out of her sight. But today, for some reason, she stared at it with an odd kind of fascination. That thing—that slug—that slimy snail with no shell was inching up the steep incline with no effort at all. It didn't have to drag along knapsacks or sleeping bags either.

"This is weird," Emily whispered. "I must be going bananas! How can I be jealous of a banana slug?"

It was one question for which she never bothered to figure out an answer. Instead, she looked away and started climbing again. She was anxious to reach Table Rock before it got too dark. Table Rock was a huge outcropping of shiny green serpentine, surrounded by a cluster of gnarled live oaks. It was a favorite spot for hikers who knew Tamalpais well, because of the spectacular views it offered of Stinson, Bolinas and the ocean.

When Emily got near Table Rock, she left her gear under a bush. Then, after checking to make sure no stray hiker was still out there reading a book of poems, she began inching along the rock ledge, flat on her stomach. "Now," she told herself, "I'll have a scratched stomach to go with my scraped fingers and legs."

Slowly, she edged her way along between trees that looked bluish in the dim light. All she wanted was one last glimpse at the two towns and ocean below, but when she looked out at the view, there wasn't any. The ocean fog was so low and dense it obscured everything farther away than one hundred feet. Emily was disappointed, and yet she was pleased to see the foggy billows swelling in the forest below her. It would be foggy on the mountain tonight but very peaceful at her secret spot.

When Emily came to the high meadows, she decided to skirt around their edges, making her way through little clusters of oak so no one would spot her out in the open. Now the walking was easier—still uphill—but not as steep. Her knapsack was on her back now with Lawrence's sleeping bag tied to it, and she was able to stride along rapidly. In fact, she found she was almost running, because it was getting dark, and she wanted to reach the cave and make camp before the last light was gone.

Even at that pace, she was able to notice the covey of quail she startled. She also saw a lot of hopping blue-bellied lizards and one slippery little grass snake. But these weren't scary—just the usual wildlife of the meadows. But then, one extraordinary thing did happen as she was hurrying along. She came over the rise of a hill looking out over a vast, empty gray-green meadow. The wind was blowing the long grasses, rippling them until, in the fading light, they looked like ocean waves, the same ones that washed in below at Stinson Beach. It was then that Emily sneezed. Maybe the pollen from the blowing grass had tickled her nose. She didn't know, but as she sneezed, suddenly, a whole herd of muletail deer rose up silently out of the grass. She rubbed at her eyes. It was like a mirage, but it was real. And, as she watched, the herd turned their white-tailed bottoms toward her and ran away noiselessly over the hills.

It was dim by the time Emily reached the cave, but she didn't care. She felt wonderful. Remembering the silent herd of deer had helped carry her along for the last half mile. Now that she had arrived, however, she tried to be quick and efficient about setting up her campsite. She unrolled Lawrence's sleeping bag on the bed of dried leaves and pine needles that covered the floor of the cave. It wasn't a deep cave—only four or five feet hollowed out into the reddish-brown rock, but it was big enough for her. And then, right beside the cave, clear, cold water bubbled out of the ground.

Carefully, Emily went through all her supplies, unpacking them and lining them up where she thought they'd be needed. She had brought matches, an extra sweatshirt, a pocket can opener, a tiny box of cereal, a Sierra Club tin cup, a can of baked beans, a package of Oreo cookies, a flashlight with new batteries. And—of course—her pencils, including Queenie.

In order to cook her dinner, she built a very small fire of dried twigs just outside the cave and next to the spring. Too much smoke might attract the attention of a ranger from a lookout on top of the mountain. Over the fire, she heated the opened can of beans. She was pleased with herself for remembering that a can would explode if it was heated unopened. As she waited for the beans to be hot enough, she sat next to the warm fire and pulled prickles out of the tops of the wool socks that stuck up out of her hiking boots.

Since she'd forgotten a spoon, she had to eat the beans by using one end of the can opener as her utensil, but she didn't care. Hot beans tasted superb because she was ravenous from her long climb. The beans filled her stomach and made her forget immediately about being tired, scratched, and achy.

When the can was empty, she filled it with spring water, heated it, and drank a canful of beany-tasting water soup. Then she refilled the can and used the water to put out the fire. When she was satisfied that there were no more dangerous embers, she opened up her pack of Oreos and sat at the edge of the water eating them one after another. She pulled each cookie apart, ate the plain side first, and then enjoyed the tastier half —the one coated with creamy white icing.

The cookies made her think of Lawrence again. He always pulled his Oreos apart. That's where she'd learned it. Her mother thought it was a disgusting habit, but her father did it, too, when he thought no one was looking.

"Lawrence won't have any Oreos tonight," Emily told herself. "In fact, without me and without Nettie, he won't have dinner at all. Maybe he'll be so worried, he won't even be hungry."

Emily had left a note for him, feeling very clever as she did so. She'd taped a little piece of paper to one of his microscope slides. Then using Queenie, who had thin retractable lead, she'd printed out a tiny message and put it in the scope.

"Nettie's at her sister's," it said. "Or at the police station in San Rafael. Call Officer Alanson." Next it said, "I've run away. Now you won't have me to annoy you any more. Don't try and find me. You never will. Signed, Emily Mendle."

Actually, it only said "Emily Mend" because she ran out of space before she got to the "le." But Lawrence was smart. He'd figure it out. "What will he do first?" she wondered. "Call Nettie's sister? The police? Call Carla?"

While she was still trying to figure this out, she reached down and flicked on her flashlight. It made an eerie glow in the fog. Instead of shining out in a long straight beam, it made only a tight little circle—a circle filled with a million or a billion little water droplets. For a minute or two, Emily just sat there fascinated, watching the currents of air move through the fog in front of her face. Then, still holding the flashlight, she stepped back to the mouth of the cave and slipped, fully clothed, into her sleeping bag.

The pencils were lying on the ground in a jumble near her head and she looked at them in the glow of the flashlight. All she saw was a bunch of old, yellow pencils—different-sized but all yellow. All yellow, she noticed, except for one shiny gold one, which reflected the beam of the flashlight, making her squint. She'd brought the pencils along because she'd been thinking about a story—about how the pencil families were abandoning civilization to set up a communal farm in Marin County. But now that she was up at the cave, she didn't really feel like working on it. She'd need to keep her flashlight on. She'd need to separate the pencils into families and stare at them in order to work out the details of the story. If she did those things, she'd just be wasting the flashlight batteries. And, besides, the bright glare reflecting from Queenie was making her head ache.

She flipped off the flashlight. Then she lay in the sleeping bag, propped up on her elbows, looking out into the absolute darkness. For a long time, she stayed that way, listening to all the little night sounds. She heard an owl. That didn't scare her. She heard the scraping noises of tiny feet. Those were field mice and shrews, and they didn't bother her either. All the nocturnal animals she never saw were out now prowling for food.

She wanted to go to sleep, but she was wide awake.

And she couldn't stop thinking about Lawrence. "What is he doing right now?" she wondered. "What is he doing to try and find me?"

Emily was wide awake in the sleeping bag. For a period of time that seemed like hours, she stayed that way, still propped on her elbows. She was thinking about her brother and about whether she should have taken off her hiking boots before she slipped into the sleeping bag for the night. She kept pretending to herself that she didn't know why she wasn't sleepy. But she knew. She was waiting for something. Warm and comfortable in the silky, down sleeping bag, she was waiting for Lawrence. Waiting for him to come crashing up the Matt Davis Trail, rushing to her through the darkness with her father's big-beam torch. She was looking forward to having him rescue her, to having him fuss over her and be very grateful he'd found her alive and safe. Carla wouldn't keep a secret. She never did. Especially from Lawrence. Carla would do anything to please him.

Emily was sure that Lawrence would yell at her when he came. He'd yell a lot, very loud, telling her how dumb she was to have run away. But maybe he'd also care enough to take the time to help her figure out about being followed and about being robbed of nothing. Lawrence was smart in a way she wasn't. She needed his help.

"What was it Nettie said on the phone today?" Emily asked herself, straining to remember. "Something about different ways of being smart?" Emily sighed. That Lawrence—he was smart in all the right ways.

She kept waiting and waiting. When her elbows got tired, she collapsed her arms to the ground and leaned her chin on her hands. But Lawrence still didn't come. Emily was beginning to feel less confident and happy than she'd felt at dinner time. Maybe she should have gone to Carla's house. If Lawrence came at that very moment, she decided, she might almost agree with him if he told her she was dumb. If Carla appeared with Lawrence and told her that thinking the pencil families would be company on the mountain was stupid and childish, she'd agree with that, too. Although she was listening intently, she could hear nothing which might suggest that Lawrence was crashing up the mountainside to save her. She began to feel very much alone. Alone and thirsty.

"That's a dumb combination," she told herself. It must have been the beans and chocolate that had made her so terribly thirsty, she thought. Her mouth was absolutely dry, and she could taste the sticky sweetness of the Oreos stuck between the bands on her teeth. She wanted a drink desperately, but still she didn't really want to crawl out in the cold darkness just to get a cup of water from the spring.

Something tickly was crawling over her hand as she thought about being thirsty and alone. An ant? A beetle? Emily brushed it away. She did want the drink, but she couldn't make herself move. As she was trying to force herself to get up, she began to be conscious of a faint, unfamiliar noise in the cave. It wasn't a mouse sound or a bug sound. It wasn't the rustle or squeak of a bat. It was a totally unfamiliar noise—a papery, crackling sound.

For a long moment, she held her breath and listened. She was trying to feel brave and confident. But she didn't. The strange, papery noise frightened her—just a little.

# 11

"You're a dummy," she told herself aloud, talking to drown out the noise. "Nothing here can hurt you." She found the sound of her voice so comforting that she kept on talking. "I think I *will* get up and get a drink . . ."

She crawled forward out of the down bag. Immediately, the night cold penetrated through her clothes making her shiver. For a moment, she considered sliding right back in the bag without any water, but then, determined, she switched on the flashlight and picked up her cup. The foggy circle of light in front of her was only about two feet wide. It was more than enough, however, to take her to the edge of the spring.

There she bent down and scooped up some water. The flashlight showed her that there was a tiny black bug swimming in the cup. But she didn't do anything about it. It seemed like too much effort to scoop up a bugless portion of water, so she gulped it down, bug and all.

"Just a little extra protein," she told herself, wondering how long the bug would keep swimming in her stomach. She was still thirsty, but she didn't drink any more because she could feel the icy spring water chilling her insides. She even thought she could feel the gulps of water dropping into her stomach and making her cold.

She was still thinking about her stomach when she first noticed that her teeth were making a strange chattering sound. Chatter-chatter. Chatter-chatter.

"That's the weirdest noise," she thought. Chatter-chatter. Then she tried clamping her jaws together to stop the noise. But it didn't stop. It kept right on going, and, suddenly, she realized that it was a louder version of the papery rustle she'd heard before. Only now as she listened hard, it didn't sound like chatter-chatter any more. It sounded like rattle-rattle.

Emily wheeled around. There on the ground at the mouth of the cave next to Lawrence's sleeping bag was a strange black and white object—almost like a curled-up bicycle tire. *It* was black and white and going rattle-rattle. Paralyzed, Emily stood there, cup in one hand and flashlight hanging limply in the other. Over and over again in the cold foggy night, the coiled-up black and white thing was going rattle-rattle.

"Lawrence! Law-rence!" Emily bellowed.

Calling for her brother on the dark, misty mountain was stupid, Emily knew that. But she simply didn't know what else to do. She did know she was absolutely alone up there—just her and the coiled rattling snake.

The end of the snake's tail was shaking so furiously that it was a blur in the flashlight beam. Emily stood rigidly only three or four feet away wondering what she ought to do. For what seemed like a long time, she just stared at the snake. She couldn't seem to see his head—no head and no red, forked tongue—only his blurry rattling tail.

"Do something," she told herself. Her teeth were really chattering now, competing with the snake sound. At last, she did the only thing she could think of. She kicked some loose pebbles at the snake. But he didn't move. He just stayed where he was, coiled and rattling.

Emily swallowed hard. "It's *my* cave," she moaned. "You're not supposed to be here. Snakes don't come out at night. You're cold blooded. You should be in some nice warm place . . ."

A nice warm place—like a cave. Emily sighed as she suddenly realized that *her* cave was *his* cave. She'd probably been sharing it with him all evening, until she slipped out to get herself a drink. "Was I worse off before in the sleeping bag?" she asked herself. "Or am I worse off now?" She didn't have any answers for her questions.

She kept on staring down at the snake. He wasn't a very big snake, actually. Maybe two or three feet long if he weren't all wound up like a spring. His body was thin and delicately criss-crossed in a black and white pattern. If she had been in the city at the Academy of Sciences looking at him through a thick pane of glass, she would have declared him to be beautiful. But she was alone in the open on the mountain, and he was only a few feet away, coiled up next to Lawrence's sleeping bag.

As she stared, she realized that the snake was terrified, too. As terrified as she was. He didn't know what to do either. For an instant, she almost felt sorry for him. But not quite sorry enough to crawl back in the sleeping bag and share the cave with him for the rest of the night.

Like a fine rain, the heavy wet fog swirled around her head. It was an impossibly dense fog. "How can Lawrence—even Lawrence—ever climb up to rescue me tonight?" she asked herself. "What do I do now?"

The rattling from the blurry tail kept going on and on without even the tiniest pause. "Stop it," Emily cried, trying to decide how long she and the snake had been there confronting each another. Maybe a minute, she decided, or two at the most. But it seemed like an hour. Or forever. She couldn't remember ever having been so terrified. Ever. Except—Sunday at the lagoon—when she'd looked down at the dead body. That had been a scary dead thing and this was a scary living one. A living thing with a poison that could make other living things dead. She didn't want to be dead on

Tamalpais with her boots on like Willard Conners at the lagoon.

"Do something," she told herself, feeling a warm panic ripple through her body. So, she did something. She threw the tin cup at the snake. She threw it as hard as she could.

He stopped rattling. Emily moved a step closer. Had she killed him? She didn't really want to do that. The snake was very still. She took one more step. But as she did, he suddenly rattled, uncoiled, and shot out at her foot.

Emily screamed. One long, loud, piercing scream. Then she turned and started to run. She stumbled through the brush until, almost by themselves, her feet found the Matt Davis Trail. "I'll follow it," she panted. "All the way down."

Fog or no fog, darkness or no darkness, she was going to run all the way down the steep path to her house. By herself. Alone. She was running in terror. Running away from a beautiful black-and-white snake that had bitten her left boot.

"Not me. Not me," she told herself thankfully as she shined her flashlight directly down and followed the three-foot-wide path across the high meadows as fast as she could. With her eyes fixed on the ground, she was running in the tiny circle of misty light that her flashlight created for her. She ran on and on, relieved to know that only her boots had been bitten. Her wonderful old muddy high-topped boots. They had saved her from being poisoned, and now they would carry her down the mountain all the way to her house.

She didn't hear any more rattling now. Only the thudding of her heavy-soled boots and her own rapid breathing. Panting, she ran on across the meadows, following the small pool of light. "This is going to be easy," she told herself. "So easy."

But, as she quickly discovered, it wasn't quite that easy. At the first fork in the brown trail, she stopped abruptly. In the darkness, she couldn't see any familiar rocks or stumps. She wasn't at all sure whether she ought to turn to the left or right. She needed her map, but it was back at the cave with the rattlesnake. To the right, she decided at last. All the trails led down eventually, but she wanted to stay on the Matt Davis, the main one. It would take her almost to her own door.

After that, she didn't run any more. She followed the path carefully out of the meadows and into the even deeper blackness of the night woods. Down and down she went, trying to step very carefully. The steeper the trail became, the harder it was to walk downhill looking only at her feet. As careful as she tried to be, her feet kept slipping and sliding. She didn't want to fall. She couldn't let herself fall and go rolling to the bottom of a gully. She might be knocked unconscious. She might roll into a whole nest of rattlesnakes. She just had to keep going, slowly and safely. One foot and then the other foot.

But it wasn't quite as simple as it sounded, because her knees had begun to quiver in a way that was most unfamiliar to her. Emily found that the quivering was making any walking difficult, much less walking down a steep incline in the dark. And yet, she didn't stop. Not for one moment. She wasn't lost. She knew right where she was—in the canyon next to the gurgling stream. She couldn't see it, but she heard it clearly and its song was reassuring. But not quite reassuring enough, she realized. She was still alone. She felt incredibly tiny, hardly bigger than a field mouse. If she had felt very proud and cocky climbing up Mount Tam, now she felt as young and dumb as Lawrence always said she was.

"I'm sorry, Lawrence," she mumbled aloud, "sorry I'm so dumb. But I'll make it back—don't worry."

She *was* going to make it. She was determined. It might take a long time, but she'd get there. And safely. She didn't notice any details on the way down. No bird sounds, no trees, no frogs, no ferns. She also didn't notice the loose slippery stone in the middle of the stream—until she slipped on it and fell, with a splat, into the cold water. Then she was wet and shivery and her bottom was bruised, adding to the cuts and scratches she'd gotten on the way up the mountain. But, whatever punishment she took bouncing into the water, she had managed as she fell to hold the flashlight high and safely out of the water. A bruised bottom didn't matter much at this point, but the flashlight did.

And, besides, she was happy to have crossed the stream. This meant she was into the lower meadow area and not far from her house. She knew how close she was getting because she began to feel the ocean wind and taste its salt on her lips. From time to time, for a moment she'd be able to see the lights winking below at Stinson as the wind swirled through the fog billows. It comforted her to know that her town was there, her home—and her brother.

If Lawrence could ever forgive her, she decided, for running away, she'd forgive him for not coming to find her. And then she'd promise never to play stupid tricks again. She just wanted to make it home and have him look after her. Wrap her cold, wet body in a warm blanket and talk to her as he had on Sunday after she'd found the body at the lagoon.

At last the dirt trail turned to gravel, and then to cement. Then she was only two blocks from her house. She could see it on the hillside ahead of her, with its lights still blazing. She didn't see any sign of a police car, but Emily knew that Lawrence must be sitting inside worrying about her. Maybe Lawrence and Nettie both. She thought she would run all the way down the street, up the steps, and just burst in through the door. Next, if Lawrence would let her, she'd hug him and hug him.

When she reached the steps, though, she changed her mind. She decided she had to peek in through the porch window, look at Lawrence and see if he seemed to be upset. She stopped running. As soon as she did, she was able to hear voices inside. She tried not to breathe so loudly. Then, as silently as she could in her hiking boots, she tiptoed up the stairs and peered in the window.

Because the curtain was pulled, she had to squint to see through its sheer whiteness. Through the criss-crossed fibers, she could see Lawrence seated on the couch with his back held very straight, instead of in its usual slouching position, and she could hear his voice talking. There were other voices, too. She couldn't see Nettie, but she did see that the others were wearing jeans. They were wearing jeans and talking in low voices to Lawrence.

Suddenly, Emily was furious. She was missing from home late at night. She'd been alone up near the top of Tamalpais, being threatened by a rattlesnake so that she'd had to run all the way down the mountain in the dark by herself. And Lawrence wasn't even looking for her. He was sitting in their living room having a party. He wasn't worried about her at all. In fact, he probably didn't know she was gone. He hadn't even noticed. Or just didn't care.

Emily lunged forward twisting the doorknob and kicking open the front door. "I hate you, Lawrence," she screamed, rushing forward fiercely and butting with her head so that she and Lawrence and the lightweight Danish couch all tumbled over backward. As she felt herself falling, she let go of the flashlight and grabbed for her brother's shirt. "I'm being bitten by a rattle-snake," she howled, "and you're having a party." They were rolling on the floor, and Emily was trying to punch him. She wanted to hurt him as she was hurting.

"Em," he pleaded, not punching back. "Stop it. This is serious."

"Who are they?" she screamed, hitting him in the chest and on the chin. "Your Shakespeare-reading group? The debating team? Are they more important than me?"

Then, without warning, Emily felt herself being lifted up from behind. Screaming and kicking, she jerked herself free from the pair of hands that was holding her and spun around. To her surprise, she found she was looking up at a boy dressed all in blue—blue jeans, blue sweatshirt. Even his face was all blue. Blue because he was wearing a knitted mask, the kind that skiers wear that covers everything but the eyes and mouth. Emily saw, surrounded by blue wool, a thin-lipped boy's mouth and a pair of dark-blue eyes with short brown lashes.

She was confused—unable to understand why Lawrence's guest would sit around the house in a ski mask. Trying to make sense of what she was seeing, Emily turned to look at the other visitors. There were two more. One was a full-breasted girl and the last was a stocky boy. These other two—they were also dressed all in blue with ski masks over their faces. Emily's first impulse was to laugh. Then she felt herself shuddering. This was no party here. Something else was going on. She turned back to Lawrence who was picking himself up from the floor.

"Emily," he said softly. "Stay calm, will you? All they want is a pencil. A gold pencil they say you stole from them. I was hoping you'd stay at Carla's, but now that you're here you must tell them what you know. Did you steal someone's pencil for your collection?"

"Where's Nettie?" Emily asked.

"At her sister's. She called at McHenrys to say she's feeling better and will be home in the morning. Now concentrate, Emily. Did you steal a gold pencil?"

She nodded. "How long have they been here?"

"Hours," Lawrence said. "Since I got home. Can you hear me, Em? Did you steal a gold pencil? If so, you must go get it right away. These people are not fooling around. I don't want either one of us to get hurt—so we must cooperate. Do you understand?"

"I did take a pencil," Emily answered, "but not from *them.*"

The tall boy grabbed her arm and squeezed it. "Where's the pencil?" he demanded. His voice seemed familiar, but Emily wasn't sure why.

"At the cave . . . on the mountain," she whispered, looking at Lawrence and at the others. "All the way at the top . . . in the cave . . . with a rattlesnake."

Almost incoherently, she found herself trying to explain about running away, about the snake, about her trip home. As she babbled on and on, she kept trying to sort out what she was looking at. She was trying to figure out if these three had something to do with being followed, with the non-robbery, with the lagoon and Willard Conners—and with Queenie. But she was so tired and she just couldn't seem to make sense out of what she was seeing. Rambling on and on, she stared at the strange trio in blue ski masks.

Then something caught her eye. Something about the large-breasted girl with greenish-blond hair sticking out from under the ski mask. The girl was holding something in her right hand. Something shiny. Small and shiny. A shiny black gun.

# 12

"We want that gold pencil, kid. Is it really in a cave on top of Mount Tam?"

Taking her eyes away from the shiny gun, Emily nodded her head at the familiar-sounding ski-masked boy. "In a cave with a rattlesnake," she echoed thoughtfully.

"You're lying!" said a tough girl-voice from behind her.

As she was spinning around to see who had just spoken, the phone started ringing. Emily wanted to run over and grab it, but she didn't move. Instead, she stood there staring at the blond girl with the gun and trying to decide why the hair curling out from under her mask looked so green.

"That phone hasn't stopped ringing all night. What's with this place?" the girl asked.

"Western Union," Emily answered. "It's probably just someone wanting to send a telegram."

"Send a telegram?"

"Yeah," she said, trying not to let the sight of the gun make her even shakier than she already was. "Our number is just like the new Western Union—except for the area code—and these people call all the time wanting to send telegrams."

"You're putting us on," said the tall boy.

Lawrence shook his head. "No, she's right. And people who dial wrong never hang up, because they're sure they have Western Union and Western Union always answers eventually."

Emily stood looking up into the masked boy's open mouth. She saw that he had a lot of silver fillings. The phone was still ringing. Ringing and ringing. "Do you want me to get it?" she asked.

The tall boy looked over at the third member of their group—the stocky, ski-masked boy. "What do you think, Bunny?"

The boy named Bunny nodded his blue-wool head and as he did Emily noticed he was wearing *her* sand dollar necklace. She wanted to say something, but she didn't. Instead, she started toward the phone.

"No funny business," said the blonde. "I do have a gun, you know."

Slowly Emily picked up the receiver, wondering who would be on the other end. The palm of her hand was sticky. She was hoping to hear her mother's voice, her father's—or even Nettie's.

"Hello," she said, talking into the phone but never taking her eyes off the three blue-faced intruders.

"Emily, is that you?" a voice squealed. It was Carla—just Carla. "I've been trying to get you all night! I thought you were running away, and I was trying to get Lawrence because he never called and I was too worried to sleep so I . . ."

"No this is *not* Western Union," Emily said. "Hang up. Dial the area code—800—first."

Then she hung up. But, before she could take her hand off the receiver, the phone started ringing again.

"Not again!" cried the blonde. "I can't stand it. And I can't stand this mask either, Bunny. It itches like hell and I think I'm allergic to wool."

"How do you get it to stop?" the masked boy asked Emily.

"I take messages. Yesterday I took one from a man named Walter. If I do that then they don't call back."

"Then do it," said the blonde, "before I have Kush rip it out of the wall."

Emily giggled nervously. "That's what they do on TV," she said, listening to the ringing and hoping it was Carla calling back, "where it's all fake. But I bet it takes a lot of muscle to pull a real phone out of the wall."

"Shut up, Emily," growled Lawrence.

"Maybe I better answer it and take the message," she said, looking back and forth between her brother and the other three. She should have felt terrified at being held captive by three masked strangers. But they just didn't seem all that scary. Lawrence was afraid, and yet —to her—it all seemed more like a pencil-family story. Like it was all pretend. Nothing seemed quite real enough to hurt her.

As she watched, the boy whose name appeared to be Kush looked for approval to the stocky silent teen-ager by the piano. Then Kush turned to Emily. "Get it," he said.

Emily lifted the phone again. "Western Union," she said slowly.

"Emily!" Carla squealed. "What's going on? What kind of dumb game are you playing now?"

"Yes, I understand, you want to send a telegram . . ."

"Emily! You're acting crazy. I'm going to wake up my mom if you don't start making sense."

"Now let me see," Emily said in her most efficient grown-up tone. Her voice had a little tremor in it which she couldn't seem to control, but she hoped the three intruders wouldn't notice that. "Your name is Mrs. Peter Dixon of 322 San Rafael Avenue in Belvedere. Yes, I've got that. Now give me your message. Slowly, please."

"Emily," Carla groaned. "Stop playing these games. Or I *will* wake up my mom—and maybe Dad, too. This isn't just a threat. I really will."

Emily nodded her head and started talking again.

" 'Peter, come home. The children need you. I do, too. Signed Melanie.' " Emily nodded her head a few extra times, staring at the strangers to see if they thought her performance was convincing.

"I hate you, Emily," Carla said, in the quiet mean voice she saved for momentous occasions. "I'm having insomnia worrying that you've run away and you're playing pencil families!"

"Thank you so much, Mrs. Dixon," Emily said sweetly. "Thank you for calling Western Union." Then, quickly so Carla's angry voice wouldn't carry across the room, she hung up.

"That's funny," Kush said, bending down and lifting the couch back onto its feet.

"Yes," Emily agreed.

Kush was chuckling. Even his chuckle was familiar. "So you just take down the messages and they never go to anyone? That really is pretty funny."

"Kush!" said the girl with the gun. She spoke, Emily noticed, in a high-pitched little voice. "We're here about the pencil—Bunny's pencil. Remember? So do something before this itching mask drives me right out of my skull."

With a shrug, Kush stopped chuckling. "Right," he agreed, his blue eyes staring at Emily through the holes in the mask. "All right, kid, so the pencil's on top of the mountain. How long will it take us to get up there?"

"With the fog? Two hours—or three," she answered, still conscious of how unreal everything seemed.

"You're lying!" said a tough-sounding girl-voice from over by the piano.

Emily squinted. This was the one the others had called Bunny. Not a stocky boy but a stocky *girl*—a girl named Bunny. All of a sudden, everything made sense to Emily. Everything she'd been too tired or too dumb to piece together faster. She knew these people—at least she knew two of them.

"Have you sold any magazines lately?" she asked Kush, wondering if the chain she saw at the edge of his neck had a sun-shaped pendant dangling from it. Then she turned to the girl called Bunny. "Where's your white fur vest?"

"That child knows who we are," whined the blonde with the gun. She was pointing it right at Lawrence, Emily noticed, but her finger wasn't on the trigger.

"I saw you at the lagoon," Emily said. "And you *must* be the ones who tore up our house because you have my necklace. You stole it!"

"Right!" snapped Bunny. "And you stole my pencil, didn't you? And I want it back. Now give it to me. It's not really on the mountain. Fork it over and we'll leave. You'll never see us again."

"Did you kill him?" Emily asked, suddenly too tired

to figure out what it was she should be saying. "Did you kill Mr. Conners?"

"Emily," Lawrence growled. "Pipe down." Then he turned to the three others. "Listen, you've got to excuse my sister. She's just a kid—a crazy dumb little kid—and she says stupid things sometimes. But I'll keep her quiet. I promise. Now, shut up, Em."

Her brother was looking out for her, giving her good advice, but it came too late because by the time he had finished speaking, Bunny was already stalking across the room. She grabbed Emily by the elbows and threw her roughly onto the couch. "Now, you listen to me, cookie, we're still asking the questions around here. And this is the question: *where is my gold pencil?*"

Shrinking back into the corner of the couch, Emily looked up at Bunny. She pulled her feet up so that her knees were under her chin. Wet knees from falling in the stream and muddy boots making streaks on the couch. "Look at me," Emily said, when she finally found her voice again. "Don't I look like I've just come down from Tam?"

"She does," Kush agreed, moving in to take a closer look. "Say, Bunny, can't we strip off these masks? They're hot and the kid knows us anyway."

"No," said Bunny. "Come on, Kush. You too, Dinah. Let's make the kid and her brother take us up to that cave right now. Then we'll grab the pencil and split."

Emily tried leaning her head back and blinking her eyes very rapidly several times. She was exhausted. She didn't know if she could stay awake—much less climb back up the mountain now. She was exhausted and beginning to feel scared. Scared for herself and for Lawrence. This was all her fault. She'd gotten the two of them into this mess. Dumb Emily.

"In this fog?" Kush said, pulling aside the curtain on the front window. "You've got to be crazy. Maybe the kid could come down in the dark, but all she had to do was go downhill. How would we find the way up to some secret cave at the top? Look at it out. It's like pea soup. And, besides, I don't like snakes."

"Me either," squeaked the girl named Dinah.

Emily tried sending a cheerful smile over toward Kush. He didn't seem like such a bad guy. He looked gruesome with the blue mask on, but he didn't talk like a thief—or like a murderer. "I'll take you up right now," she offered. "But it'll start to get light in about five hours and then it would be easier because we wouldn't have to worry about getting lost."

Kush liked her idea. His blue eyes opened wider and his mouth glinted with silver as he grinned. Bunny wasn't so easily convinced, however, and she began to argue with her two friends in loud, firm tones. Emily sat on the couch next to Lawrence, listening to Bunny trying to persuade Dinah and Kush to go get the pencil immediately. As she listened, she kept looking at Kush's silver fillings and wondering when thieves had time to go to the dentist.

While the three of them were going at it, Lawrence suddenly reached out and squeezed Emily's shoulder—gave it a gentle squeeze. Emily couldn't remember the last time he'd done *that*. But, still, she couldn't let herself relax and enjoy his concern now. She didn't deserve any such consideration. It was her fault they were in danger, and she had to get them out of it.

On and on they argued—the three ugly, blue faces. Emily watched them, bending her wet knees under her chin and rocking back and forth. She never let her eyes stray far from the shiny black gun. "What should I do?" she asked herself. "Will Carla send help?" No, probably not, she decided.

Then, finally, the beginnings of an idea stirred in Emily's head. It was such a good idea that she sat up straight and was willing to interrupt the argument.

"Would you like some pop?" she called out, looking from one wool mask to the other.

Kush shook his head. "No pot. We never touch the stuff. None of us. It messes up your head."

Emily laughed and stood up. "Not *pot*—pop. Like

*soda pop*? Aren't you thirsty? I'm terribly thirsty because I had this can of beans and Oreos . . ."

"Yeah, yeah," said Bunny. "You told us that already. No, we don't want pot or pop either!"

Emily sat back down. "Well, I just thought you might like something while you're talking about when we should go for the pencil."

"Okay," Bunny agreed. "Shut up and get us something. Anything."

"What do you have?" Kush asked pleasantly.

Emily leaned her head to one side. What did everything going on in her house have to do with a dead body in the lagoon, she wondered? Except for the ski masks, these three were such ordinary people. They didn't seem like murderers—or even like thieves—except for those masks. "Well," she said, starting to answer Kush, "we have . . ."

"Where do you think we are, Kush?" Bunny griped. "Perry's Bar and Grill? Just bring what you have."

"How about homemade root beer?" Emily asked slowly.

"I love root beer," Dinah piped up.

"Okay, okay—root beer," Bunny said. "Just get it. But we'll be watching you. Stay where we can see you. And remember we'll have that gun pointing at your brother's head."

Emily shot a quick look at Lawrence. He was sitting

stiffly, looking exhausted, Emily decided. Tired and frightened. "Is he working on a plan, too?" she wondered.

Moving slowly, she stood up again. She tried to give Lawrence a little wink, but her eye sort of twitched instead. "I'll have to go to the back pantry for the root beer," she said.

"Is there a door there?"

"No," declared Emily. "But you should know that. You tore all through this place, didn't you?"

"Emily, that's enough," Lawrence said sternly. "Stop playing games. I promised we'd cooperate. Now keep your mouth closed and do as you're told. Go and get them the root beer, will you?"

Without answering her brother, Emily headed toward the pantry. She was almost there when the phone started ringing.

"Another call for Western Union?" Dinah asked. "This sure is one crazy house."

"Come back and get it, cookie," Bunny ordered, as she reached up to scratch under the edge of her evil-looking mask.

Nodding obediently, Emily backtracked and went to pick up the phone. "Hello," she said, wondering whose voice she'd hear this time, "Western Union."

"Emily, it's me again—Carla. I don't hate you—really I don't. And I didn't wake up my mom. But I still can't get to sleep. Is something wrong over there? Your voice sounds funny, and you never play a dumb game like Western Union without starting to laugh and ask me if you weren't terrific. Were you trying to tell me something before with that message about Mrs. Dixon?"

"Yes," Emily answered, trying to sound as casual as she could. "Yes, I did, Mrs. Dixon. I sent off your message right away."

"Yes, you mean, *yes?*" Carla asked.

"Yes, ma'am."

"What should I *do?*"

"Thank you for calling Western Union," she said, craning her head to see if the gun was still pointing at Lawrence. It was. "And, believe me, Mrs. Dixon, we're very reliable."

Hoping Carla understood, Emily hung up. She was sure she had sounded strange, but she didn't know if she'd sounded strange enough to make Carla do something. Call someone. Send someone to rescue them.

"Get much of that?" Kush asked.

"Much of what?" she asked nervously.

Kush rolled up the bottom part of his mask, uncovering his mouth and chin. "People calling back?"

As Emily was staring down at her ragged fingernails groping for an answer, Lawrence spoke up. "Yes, as a matter of fact we do. Sending telegrams seems to make people worry. So they call again to be reassured."

She was relieved that Lawrence had come to her rescue. She gave him a little thank-you nod. That was all she could manage with the others watching her. Then she headed for the back pantry again. Kush was following her. His heavy desert boots came clomping across the floor behind her. "Say, Emily, how do you make homemade root beer?" he asked.

She stopped and looked back at him. "We get a kit—made by Hires—and add distilled water and sugar."

"Kush!" Bunny commanded. "We're not here to exchange recipes. All I want is that pencil. And the sooner the better. Waiting 'til morning will be a mistake."

With a little smile on her face, Emily went back into the pantry alone. She was glad Bunny had called for Kush. She didn't want him breathing down her neck while she fixed the drinks. First, she lined up five glasses, listening to the drone of voices as she did so. It sounded as if Bunny was going to win and they'd all be climbing uphill in the dark fog. Root beer might quench their thirsts, but it wasn't going to make them feel warm as they climbed. They needed something, she decided, to make them feel warm.

She had three tall green glasses with a bamboo pattern on the sides and two short, clear jelly-jar glasses. Into each one, she put two ice cubes. After that, she reached down and lifted the big gallon jug off the floor.

She filled the two clear glasses right up to the top

with homemade root beer. When she got around to pouring it into the green glasses, however, she only filled them two-thirds full. Then, making sure no one in the living room could see her, she grabbed another bottle off the shelf—a bottle full of a clear liquid. Each of the green glasses got filled up to the top with the clear liquid.

Emily stirred these three glasses thoroughly. Then she carried them into the other room and served them to Dinah, Bunny and Kush. After they were served, she brought out the two smaller glasses—one for her and one for Lawrence.

Sitting down next to her brother on the couch, she handed him one of the glasses. She was sitting very close to him, closer than she'd been allowed to sit for at least two years. She could feel his reassuring warmth next to her arms as she held the glass of root beer in front of her.

Lawrence didn't say anything, but he did give her a questioning look, raising his right eyebrow. Emily wanted to answer. She wanted him to know exactly what she'd done, yet she felt she couldn't risk being overheard by the three masked visitors.

"Terrific root beer," Kush was telling her. "The best I've ever had. You have any more?"

"Plenty," Emily assured him, pulling on one of her damp tangled ponytails. "Lawrence likes my root beer, too, so I always make a lot at one time."

"Doesn't anyone ever call you Larry?" Kush asked him.

"No," said Lawrence.

"Poor guy," Kush said, turning away to listen to a question Dinah was asking about snakes.

Emily could feel herself beginning to relax a little. She looked at the gun. It was sort of hanging from one of Dinah's fingers as she drank the root beer. It didn't look as dangerous that way. But there was another reason that she didn't feel quite as frightened. These three in ski masks who wanted a pencil she'd stolen from a bag washed up near a dead body were probably thieves and maybe even murderers, but still Emily rather liked them. She liked them for one specific reason. It had taken a long time, but at last she'd found some people dumber than she was. Not just one—but three of them—in the same place at the same time, taking all kinds of risks just to recover a gold pencil.

Sitting there on the couch, Emily sipped her drink and watched the other three drink theirs. She was sitting very close to her brother, pulling on one ponytail and feeling, for once, very smart.

"Nettie's vodka," she whispered to Lawrence, pulling her pony tail across her mouth for camouflage. "In *their* root beer."

# 13

"Why don't elephants join the police force?" Emily asked Kush.

"Why? Why?" he laughed.

"Because they don't hide behind billboards very well."

Kush laughed so hard he managed to spill some of his second drink. Dinah giggled. Even Bunny smiled.

Root beer and vodka had made these three very jolly. They had even agreed to peel off the ski masks, since drinking liquid through the tight mouth openings had proved to be a rather soggy procedure. Now the masks were thrown on the floor with all the other debris.

"Wait, wait," Dinah tittered. "I have one. It's my turn now. What's wrinkled and goes slam-slam-slam-slam?"

"A four-door prune!" Emily scoffed. "That's an old one. Really old. Everyone knows that. But I have something to ask—not a joke, just something I want to know. Why does Dinah's hair look so green? Why, Dinah? How come?"

"Because I swim," Dinah said. "I race and the chlorine from the pool turns my hair green."

"What's green and goes splash-splash-splash-splash?" Kush asked.

"Dinah!" Emily shouted out.

"No," chuckled Kush. "That's wrong. It's Moby Pickle."

It had been a long time since anyone in the room had mentioned climbing Tamalpais in the dark, and Emily was doing everything she could to keep the subject from coming up. When the exchange of elephant jokes began to bog down, she was ready with another idea.

"Listen," she said, jumping up from the couch. "How about some entertainment? Real entertainment. I'll play the piano, okay?"

Without waiting for any answers, she ran over and sat down on the piano bench. Then she launched into her fastest, loudest rendition of the "Spinning Song." She was about to run through it for a second time, when she found that she was being nudged over on the piano bench. To her surprise, it was Bunny doing the pushing.

"It's my turn," Bunny insisted. "I used to be into all this piano stuff, too, you know, when my folks were still trying to turn me out cultured. What do you want? 'Country Gardens'?"

"Hey, I play that," Emily said. "Why don't we play it together—in different octaves?"

They tried it. Emily could hardly play she was so amazed to see tough, short-haired Bunny with her stubby fingers flying gracefully over the keys. When they had played "Country Gardens" through twice, Bunny pushed Emily the rest of the way off the piano bench. Then she began rolling up her sleeves. "And now, Ladies and Gentlemen, to conclude our special midnight concert, I shall give you the 'Minute Waltz' in fifty-nine seconds."

Kush timed her playing with the second hand of his watch. The first time it took three and a half minutes. The second time Bunny managed to run through it in two minutes and fifty seconds. After an equally futile third try, Bunny gave up and asked Emily for another root beer. "I used to be able to do it," she kept saying. "What's happened to me?"

"After I get the root beer, can I try on one of the masks?" Emily asked Bunny. "Where did you get them anyway? And the gun?"

"At Kush's house. He used to ski."

"Ski? Do robbers ski?"

"Emily . . ." Lawrence pleaded.

Bunny laughed. "We're not robbers," she said, "even if we did come here dressed up in those stupid masks. We go to school—just like you and your brother—only in the city. Kush and I graduate this year and Dinah next January. We're not robbers. We just hang out over here because we like the beach . . . and we like action. There's always something going on over here, and we just like to get in on it if we can. Now, get me that soda, will you?"

Emily never quite got a chance to try on a mask. She was kept too busy running back and forth, filling green glasses with root beer and vodka. As she refilled them, she kept wondering if Bunny had told the truth and wondering—since no one had answered her question—just where the gun had come from.

She tried to keep an eye on it as she hurried between the pantry and the living room. She wanted to do something to get rid of it, but she didn't know quite what. It wouldn't do any good, she decided, to try and grab it and run. There were three of them against only Emily and Lawrence. Besides, all three of them were bigger and tougher-looking than either of the Mendles. Emily hadn't given up hope that Carla would do something. Maybe. But, in the meantime, she had to keep waiting and watching—watching Dinah because she was holding the gun and Bunny because she seemed to be in charge.

Bunny didn't play the piano anymore, but she kept sitting on the piano bench. For a long time she sat there staring into her glass. Then she spoke. "What are we doing here? Waiting for it to get light. And why? Why did we get into this whole thing in the first place? For excitement. Ha! To chase down a stupid pencil. What do I need the pencil for? I don't even need it, and here I am waiting around to climb a mountain to get it back. That's the funniest thing I've ever heard." No one else laughed at Bunny's words, but she rocked back and forth snickering to herself.

Emily watched this for a moment. Then she turned to Kush who was sitting nearby on the floor. "What's so important about the pencil?" she asked quietly.

His answer was prompt, but his voice was extremely loud. It seemed to echo into every corner of the Mendle house. "It has Bunny's name on it and she wants it back."

Leaning forward so her face was right next to Kush's, Emily asked another question. She was hoping his next reply would be softer. "What does the pencil have to do with the body?"

She was almost whispering, but, still, Lawrence heard her. "Shut up," he said. "Shut up and drink your pop."

Emily took a big gulp of root beer, knowing Lawrence was right and half hoping Kush wouldn't answer. But he did, and this time his voice was even louder. "Hey, Bunny, did you hear that? Little Tinselteeth here wants to know what the pencil has to do with the body."

Emily squirmed. "Forget it," she mumbled. "I don't want to know. Really I don't. I'm sorry I asked."

Bunny stood up, crossed the room, and slumped down

in the desk chair in front of Lawrence's microscope. "No, it's okay," she said without any particular emotion. "We didn't kill him, if that's what you mean."

Running one hand through her curly hair, still mashed from being under a ski mask for so many hours, she kept on talking. "We didn't kill him and we don't know anything about any of that stuff. Nothing."

"Nothing," echoed Kush.

"Sunday we had a picnic on the island. Okay? Just a picnic, and by mistake, I left my bag there. We were coming back to find it when you started yelling your head off."

"Well, what about Willard Conners?" Emily asked.

"What about him, cookie? Are we guilty of something because his body washed up near my bag? I'd never laid eyes on him before—like I'd never laid eyes on you until I saw you ripping off my pencil."

"She's telling the truth," Dinah squeaked. "Really she is."

"If we did know anything about that guy's death, would we have been hanging around there?" asked Kush.

"Why should I believe you?" Emily said, trying to ignore the fact that Lawrence was giving her meaningful kicks with the toe of his left sneaker. "How do I know you're not lying—that you didn't really rob the house and kill Mr. Conners?"

"Emily!" Lawrence pleaded. "Button your lip."

Bunny shrugged. "No, it's all right. Let her talk."

Encouraged, Emily continued. "You broke into our house and stole my sand dollar necklace, didn't you?"

"Yes . . . yes, we did," Bunny agreed. "We did it but I'm sick and tired of hearing you yak about it so—here—take it back, will you?"

Emily reached out for the necklace and slipped it over her head. "So that body just *happened* to wash up near your bag?"

"Yes . . . yes, it did."

Kush leaned forward. "That's the west side of the island—the part that gets the afternoon sun—and the shore where the tide washes things up."

"I found a dead pelican there once," Dinah said.

Emily frowned. "But you still could be lying. I tell a lot of lies. Ask my brother. Nettie—the crazy lady who's staying with us—she tells lies, too. Maybe you're lying."

"Maybe I am," Bunny answered, rubbing at her face again. "You're nobody anyway. I don't care if you believe me or not. I've told the truth. So take it or leave it."

"Well," Emily began. "Well . . . but . . ."

"Listen, I'll tell you one more time, cookie—and that's it," Bunny warned. "So there was this bloated body on the island and we were looking at it and you were looking at it—only you were holding my pencil, see? So we followed you—so we looked through your house. We were just trying to get my pencil back. It was just for fun—a caper like *The Sting*—for fun and because we didn't have anything better to do. And because I was afraid you might end up giving that pencil to the police and they'd think I knew something about Conners because of my name being on it and all. Blythe Queen. Ha! What a name. Did you ever know anyone who had a name like Blythe or Gay or Joy who fitted that name? Not only did my mother lay that name on me—but then she even had it engraved on a stupid pencil . . ."

"That Bunny," Dinah said with a yawn. "She's so stubborn. She gets an idea in her head and she never lets go." Dinah yawned again. "Like thinking she *has* to have that pencil back . . . ."

Listening to Dinah, Bunny and Kush made Emily feel so confused that she didn't know what to believe. Tonight they had come to her house with ski masks and a gun. Before that they'd been following her and had even broken into her house. But they still said they weren't robbers or murderers and didn't know anything about Willard Conners's death. It seemed like another pencil-family story. It seemed unreal. And Bunny wasn't at all pleasant any more.

"Want some more root beer?" Emily asked her nervously.

"No—all I want is my pencil."

Because Bunny's moodiness was disturbing to Emily, she tried to think of something lighter to discuss. "Why did the elephant wear blue tennis shoes?" she asked, pulling on one ponytail.

"I'm tired of those stupid jokes," Bunny declared. She was rubbing at her face again. It was a flat face, Emily noticed, with a large mouth, large teeth and a tiny little too-small nose. A trembly nose—like a bunny's. But not at all like a queen's. Or a Blythe Queen's.

Emily's thoughts were interrupted by a little snorting sound from the corner where Dinah was sitting. Emily looked up. Dinah's head was jerking up and down as if she could hardly keep her eyes open. The gun was dangling from one finger now. Emily stared at it, thinking that with one quick move she might be able to grab it. Grab it and point it at the three intruders while Lawrence phoned for help. But she didn't try it. There was something wrong with the idea. She didn't know anything about guns. She'd never seen a real one close up before. Trying to figure something out, she stared at it.

Apparently Bunny saw what Emily was seeing. "Take the gun, Kush," she ordered. "And give it to me."

Kush got up and did as he was told. Now, to Emily's dismay, Bunny was holding the gun and pointing it right at Lawrence's head. She was looking very mean. Not at all like the girl who'd tried to play the "Minute

Waltz" in fifty-nine seconds. Now her face had a set look.

"Would you like to hear about my pencil families?" Emily asked Kush, still watching Bunny as she spoke.

"Pencil families?" Kush laughed. His laugh was loud and strange. He was looking at Emily through the wrong end of the Mendles' binoculars.

Emily nodded. "Yeah, I collect them—the pencils—of all sizes and I write stories about them. Not on paper—just in my head. I can't show you because they're all up in that cave, but I can sort of tell you a little. Like about Mrs. Ticonderoga. I've been having this terrible problem with her. Just after the judge found her not guilty of killing her brother, she was caught trying to smuggle pot across the Mexican border. But she didn't do it, Kush. You see, she was just on her way back from a trip to Tijuana with the orphans—she was always good to the orphans—and she was framed. Framed by her brother's widow . . ."

"Pencil families? That's funny. Really funny," Kush interrupted.

"Pencils, pencils," Bunny muttered, "if you hadn't—"

The rest of her sentence was drowned out by the ringing of the phone. Emily glanced up at the clock. It was almost two. Could that be Carla again? Emily looked over at Lawrence. Then, slowly, she stood up. In order to answer the phone, she would have to walk right next to the gun. Lawrence was frowning at her and shaking his head. He was reaching out to take hold of her arm. But she *had* to answer it. It might be someone offering help. Or it might only be someone calling for Western Union.

"I'll get it," Bunny said, but she didn't. She just sat next to it, letting it ring, and rubbing at her face. After ten or twelve rings, she changed her mind. "You get it," she commanded, gesturing toward Emily.

For a moment Emily stood there listening to the chorus of piercing rings and letting Lawrence squeeze her arm. Then, pulling away from him, she started walking toward the desk where Bunny sat with the gun. The gun was held firmly in her hand, and Emily was close enough to see the little opening in front. When she picked up the phone, she'd be close enough to touch it. Close enough to grab hold of it. Maybe she should grab it and give Lawrence a chance to escape. She owed him that. This was all her fault for stealing a pencil that didn't belong to her.

But, still, she hesitated. There was something about the gun that puzzled her. Something strange about it. She'd never seen a gun before and yet, at the same time, she was absolutely sure she'd seen this one. Like in a dream somewhere.

"Maybe I have ESP," she told herself as she reached

for the telephone. "No, probably not. I never had it before . . ."

Her hand was on the receiver now only inches away from the gun. The phone was still ringing insistently. Feeling its vibrations in her fingers, through her hand, and all the way up her arm, Emily looked right into Bunny's eyes. Then, looking back at the gun, she made a decision.

"I'm not afraid of you," she told Bunny calmly. She was calm because she'd finally figured something out. Something very important.

"And I'm not afraid of your gun either," she said, taking hold of it and wrenching it out of Bunny's hand. "It can't hurt. See? It can't hurt me because—*you forgot to bring your darts.*"

Then, taking a deep breath and turning her back on Bunny, Emily lifted the receiver to her ear. "Hello, Carla? Is that you?" she asked, trying to ignore the frantic shuffling noises behind her, trying to ignore Lawrence shouting "Get out of here!" and Kush yelling "Wake up, Dinah! Wake up!"

"Yes, of course, it's *me,*" Carla squealed. "Who else would be calling you at this time of night? Is that you? What's going on there? Are you all right? What's all that commotion?"

"Oh, *that,*" said Emily. "Well . . . there are these

three kids here—three kids who've been hanging around and trying to scare us with a gun. But we're okay . . ."

As she was saying "okay" she could hear the front door being opened—opened and slammed shut again—hard.

"You see, Car-Car, their gun is just like Rob McHenry's, and it came from the 7-Eleven."

# 14

"What do you mean, Ma? What do you mean my voice sounds funny?" Emily yelled into the phone. "It's just me. You said the same thing when you talked to Lawrence."

"Well, then . . ." Joan Mendle said hesitantly, speaking from a motel somewhere in Oregon, "why don't you put Nettie on?"

"I can't," Emily answered. "She's at the beauty parlor getting a new dye job."

"You're *sure* everything's all right, dear?"

Emily glanced over at Lawrence who was seated across from her at the desk by the front window. He'd finished talking on the phone and returned to his microscope. He was busy spinning the dial and peering down at something on a little glass slide.

"Fine, fine," she assured her mother. "Everything's the same as always. Lawrence has to go to the city tonight to be interviewed by the judges. That means he'll win something—a third or second or maybe even a first prize. Mrs. Tock said she'd drive him. But everything else's the same . . ."

"Well, then . . . we'll see you Saturday. Two more days. I can't wait. Would you like to have dinner in the city after we see Lawrence's exhibit? Would you like that? Start thinking about what you'd like to wear. I bet you've grown a lot in five weeks, Em. Grown and changed."

"No. No," Emily insisted, still watching Lawrence. "I told you already—everything's the *same!*"

As soon as her mother and father had both said their good-byes, Emily dropped the telephone and turned back to the yellow tablet in front of her. A large legal-sized tablet Lawrence had bought for her in the 7-Eleven after they came back from the cave with the pencils.

Thoughtfully, Emily picked up Mrs. Ticonderoga—Mrs. Alexandra Ticonderoga—from the desk. She was sitting in a chair pulled up opposite Lawrence. She put the point of the pencil against the first blue line on the first sheet of yellow paper and waited for something to happen—for the story to start writing itself. But nothing happened. Mrs. Ticonderoga just stood there, on her head, leaning against Emily's fingers.

Looking away from the tablet, Emily gazed out the window at the late afternoon sun and the haze over the lagoon. Maybe this wasn't a good day for writing, she decided, as she looked out. Too many other things had been going on. Besides hiking up to the cave, she'd been busy talking to Carla, welcoming Nettie home, explaining to Nettie about Dinah, Kush and Bunny, listening to Nettie's stories about Officer Alanson, and calling Carla back to tell her what Nettie had said. And then, she'd had to talk to her parents, too. All of this on very little sleep.

"Did you believe them?" Emily asked, turning back toward Lawrence.

Lawrence didn't answer.

"Did you believe them?" she repeated.

Shaking the hair from his face, Lawrence looked up. "Who?"

"Kush . . . Dinah . . . Bunny?"

Looking up, he nodded. "Yes, I did and I do. Don't you? But—now—I'd like to go back to work if . . ."

"If what?"

". . . if you'll let me borrow one of your pencils."

Without hesitation, Emily rolled the whole Ticonderoga family and Queenie over to his side of the desk. "Sure. Take your pick," she said, beginning to examine her fingernails. They were dirty and strange-looking. Half of them were still long—uncut for six weeks—and the others were broken at various lengths from climbing Mount Tam and other activities. "I believe them, but there's one thing that still bothers me."

"What?"

"Well . . . I'd like to return Queenie—I mean—the gold pencil. It really doesn't belong to me, but I don't know how to send it back. I looked in the San Francisco phone book and there are *twelve* Queens—only eleven if I don't count the Queen Bee Bakery. How am I supposed to figure out which Queen is the right one?"

"I don't know, Em."

Emily frowned. "Well, I could start calling, I guess, and asking for Blythe. Or for Bunny. Maybe I'll do that . . ."

"Maybe before you do that, you should do something with that tablet I bought you. Write a story—a real story about what's happened to you in the last week. Did I make a special trip to the store and spend my baby-sitting money for nothing?"

Leaning forward, Emily let her chin rest on the tablet and her ponytails cover up the blank page. "I will. I can call tomorrow," she said. "I *will* write. Right now! But maybe I should try a different pencil." She reached out and grabbed Mrs. Ticonderoga's son Daniel. Then she put his head against the first line of the tablet. But Daniel didn't write anything either.

After a long moment, she looked at Lawrence again. He was peering into his microscope, taking rapid notes on his own yellow tablet, covering every inch of the page with indecipherable little scribbles. Sighing, she stared at her ragged fingernails again and then back at the lagoon. It was, she noticed as she picked up the binoculars and peered through them, at that incredible moment of low tide when the water flow at the narrow lagoon neck was about to change direction and begin flowing in from the ocean again. As far as she could see in both directions, there were mudflats covered with flocks of birds. Emily thought she'd never seen the lagoon quite as empty as it was at that very moment.

"Everything is different today," she told herself as she continued to stare at the empty lagoon. "And still—like I told Ma—everything *is* the same."

Yes, she'd helped rescue Lawrence—saved him and herself from more hours of being held captive. She'd saved them both by knowing, at last, that the shiny black gun was a toy from the 7-Eleven store. And she'd apologized profusely for her pranks and for causing so much trouble. But Lawrence had never said anything to her. Not a word of thanks. He was the same serious, self-absorbed, untalkative person. Even hiking up to the cave and back he'd hardly said a word. Just "Thanks, Em," would have been quite sufficient—even if he'd mumbled it.

He hadn't said one single thing about the pencils either. How she'd brought them back from the cave and selected a home for each family, instead of hiding them back under her mattress. Her eyes hopped around the room as she looked for each of the families. The Dixons were in a jar by the bulletin board. The Campus family was in a basket on the dining table and the Ticonderogas were right in front of her on the desk. She couldn't see the Eberhard-Fabers because they were by the phone in her parents' bedroom. She couldn't see the orphans either. She'd left half of them in her room and half on the night stand next to Lawrence's bed.

Emily wasn't planning to give up on the pencils entirely. She'd still keep track of them and of their stories. She'd still try to keep the families from being separated. That wouldn't be easy either. She knew that. From where she sat, she could already see that a red orphan named Venus Patriotic had somehow been thrown into the Dixon-family jar.

She sighed. Last night, for once, she'd felt so smart. This morning, too. But not now—especially since no words would write themselves on her tablet. Discouraged, she tried changing pencils again. Putting down Danny Ticonderoga, she picked up his younger sister Christina. But Emily was disappointed to find that Christina didn't have anything to say either. The page stayed entirely blank because Christina wanted to hop on her bicycle and pedal to the mouth of the lagoon to be there for the exact instant that the tide changed, to see the water flowing in from the sea again. Emily frowned. Was it Christina Ticonderoga who wanted to watch the tide change or Emily Mendle? Emily, of course. She didn't want to be here with Lawrence who didn't appreciate her even enough to say thanks.

Abruptly, she stood up. "I'm going out," she announced, fully expecting to be ignored.

To her surprise, however, Lawrence looked up immediately. "No, you're not. I want you to stay here."

Emily chewed the edge of one ragged fingernail. "Why?" she asked.

"Because," he said, resuming his furious scribbling.

"Because isn't an answer," she told him. "You don't want me here, anyway. You don't even look at me. You don't talk to me."

"I do," he yelled. "I *do* talk to you. I do look at you. I even bought you a present, didn't I? A tablet! That yellow tablet there in front of you. And I'd *love* to talk to you—especially in about an hour, after the sun sets. But I need the rest of the natural light to finish analyzing this water sample from the spring next to the cave. Now, sit down, right there in the chair across from me where I can see you. And write! You said you wanted a tablet to write on. Well, you have it. Now—*write!*"

Emily sat back down again. "I want to write," she moaned. "But I don't know how to begin. I don't have any first sentence. I don't know what to say."

With a pained expression on his face, Lawrence looked up one more time. "How about 'As the sun sinks slowly in the West'? That's an appropriate first line."

Emily nodded. "Hey, that's terrific," she agreed, looking out beyond the lagoon at the yellow-orange haze where the sun was hovering over the western horizon. " 'As the sun sinks slowly in the West.' That's good, Lawrence. Very original. Thanks. I'll use it."

Emily was just about to write the capital letter A in the word "As" when the phone started ringing. "Get it, Lawrence," she said. "I'm busy."

"You get it," he ordered. "Because I'm busy, too. I've found something important here. Something I might be able to add to my science project before the judging on Saturday. No one ever calls me anyway. It's probably Carla, and I'm not going to answer it. Now—get it!"

With another deep sigh, Emily reached out for the phone. Nothing was changed, she told herself, nothing.

"Hello," she said listlessly.

"This is Western Union," a woman's voice said.

"No, no, it isn't," Emily shouted into the phone. "You've dialed wrong. Dial again—but use the area code 800 first. This is *not* Western Union. This is the Mendle house."

As Emily was about to slam down the phone, the voice on the other end spoke again. "No, this is Western Union calling for Emily Mendle. I have a telegram here for a Ms. Emily Mendle. Is Ms. Mendle there?"

Emily pushed her left ponytail out of the way and clamped the receiver tightly against her ear. "Carla, is that you?"

"No," replied the voice on the other end. "This is Western Union calling for Emily Mendle."

"Really?"

"Really!"

"Well, I'm Emily Mendle. This isn't a joke? You have a *telegram* for *me?*"

"That's right," the woman answered. "If you have a pencil to jot down the message, I'll read it to you."

Emily grabbed for a pencil. "Okay. Go on," she said. "I'm ready . . ."

"Okay," said the woman. "Here it is." As she dictated the message, Emily wrote it all down. Then she hung up the phone and looked at what she'd written on the first page of the yellow pad.

Dear Emily,
Nettie says I'm the dumbest smart person she's ever met and you're the smartest dumb person. I think she's right. You may be an intolerable, spoiled, loudmouth brat, but you are my sister. Thanks for everything.

Sincerely,

Lawrence Mendle

P.S. How did you know it was a dart gun?

After a very long time, Emily looked up from the

message on the tablet. She could feel a wide grin stretching itself across her face. She wanted to jump up, rush around the desk, and hug her brother. But she didn't. She forced herself to stay seated in the chair opposite him. "Lawrence, did you really send this? Did you send a *real* telegram?"

"Shut up," he said, one eye squeezed shut and the other staring down into the microscope.

Emily read through the Western Union message again. Then she looked at her fingernails—then out at the lagoon. While she'd been yelling at Lawrence, answering the phone, writing down the message, the tide had changed. From where she sat she couldn't actually see the difference, but she didn't bother to pick up the binoculars because she knew it had happened. Now the water was flowing in at the mouth of the lagoon as swiftly as it had been flowing out only twenty minutes before.

"Lawrence," Emily said, looking back at her fingernails.

He didn't answer.

For a few minutes, Emily just sat there without moving. At last, when she couldn't sit still any longer, she reached for the shiny gold pencil. She picked it up and rolled it around between her fingers, twisted it to adjust the length of the lead. Then, leaning forward, she pressed the pencil against the top line of the second page of the tablet.

"Terrified," she wrote, "I looked away from the bloated body and caught sight of something shiny. . . ."

## About the Author

Susan Terris is the author of many popular books for young adults. Among them are *Whirling Rainbows, Plague of Frogs, Pickle,* and *The Drowning Boy*. A graduate of Wellesley College, she has also received an M.A. in English Literature from San Francisco State College.

Susan Terris and her husband David, a stockbroker, live in San Francisco with their three children, Danny, Michael, and Amy. For recreation, they often hike and explore on Mount Tamalpais, at Stinson Beach, and at Bolinas—the areas which provide the setting for *The Pencil Families*.